Missing
and other short stories

Penny Luker

First published in 2008 by Bindon Books, Leyton, Chester Road, Cheshire, CW6 9JA.

ISBN   978-0-9559896-0-5

Photographs by David and Penny Luker

Note from the Author

This collection of short stories is the result of a number of writing courses I have taken with the Open University, The London School of Journalism and Mid-Cheshire College. The stories cover a variety of genres, so if one doesn't appeal, it's still worth trying out the next. They are all entirely fiction and none of the events or characters is real or is based on real life.

The stories range from fantasy to ghost stories and there's even one (tongue in cheek) horror story. There are also some gentler stories, which may make you smile. I hope you find something to enjoy, but if you don't, remember you've helped to raise some money for WaterAid.

I would like to thank my family who give me encouragement to write and my tutors, who have set such interesting tasks. I'd also like to thank Linda Bond and Lynn Everott for their help and guidance and the Nantwich and District Soroptimists, www.soroptimist-gbi.org who have offered to support this project to raise money for WaterAid.

It seems to me unbelievable that in a modern world that any human being should not have easy access to fresh, safe drinking water. WaterAid has made huge progress in helping provide clean water in areas where it is scarce, but there is still more to do.

I am also a Writings Editor at the e-zine All Things Girl, so if you like reading short stories and poetry why not visit www.allthingsgirl.net. It's free!

Index

Ice

The new Lord Carmichael had just lost his father and now faced the biggest dilemma of his life. Should he sacrifice his own luxury and comforts to find the truth behind his late father's instructions or should he blindly follow the instructions as his father had done and his father before him?

On the first of every month he had to supply large quantities of food and toiletries and when requested significant amounts of materials and clothes. These he had to load onto a conveyor belt in a hidden part of the cellar. The conveyor belt went downwards. On the second of every month a small wooden box came up from the cellar filled with milky white stones. These were uncut diamonds. They were the backbone of the family's fortune and could be relied upon without fail.

Lord Carmichael reasoned that if this arrangement had been going on for four generations then whatever the arrangements were, they must be acceptable and yet something within him worried that they were not....and nagged and wouldn't rest.

Why would there be a need for food and clothes if there were not people living underground, mining the diamonds? He remembered how Europeans in Australia had hunted the Aborigine people for sport, defending their actions by saying the native population were not really humans and he knew he could never be a part of something like that.

Tomorrow was the first of the month and he sat down to write a letter.

Dear Sirs,
I wish to come down with the supplies and meet you.
Please let me know if that is agreeable to you.
Lord Carmichael

He placed the letter on the conveyor belt and pressed the button.

Early the next morning he went to load the supplies and found a reply.

Dear Lord Carmichael,

If you do come we would make you most welcome, but I must point out you would become our permanent guest.
Before you come you would need to appoint your brother to do your duties.

Respectfully

Kelman Simms.

Lord Carmichael thought about the reply long and hard. It seemed somewhat threatening. Also did he want to hand everything over to his brother? Yet still he felt uneasy as he loaded 100 packets of toilet rolls and four cases of cornflakes onto the conveyor belt. It took him one hour of physical hard work for all the supplies to be sent down out of the cellar. He added a note.

Maybe next month.
Lord C.

As expected the next day the little box came up from the depths filled to the brim with hard, large, milky stones and a little note.

We will look forward to it.
K.S.

Life continued pretty much as usual for William Carmichael. There was good food, friends to share meals with, golf and the theatre. He had no real wants or needs, just an occasional trip to the jewellers to check his profits. Of course there was many a night without sleep while he worried about the people who mined the diamonds.

When the next month came he sent another note.

Please explain why I have to become a permanent guest?
Could I just visit? I want to find out whether you want to stay where you are or whether you want to stop mining?
I'm worried about how you can stay healthy without sunlight.
Please let me know.
William Carmichael.

As he went down to load the supplies the next day, there was a note in reply.

> With due respect Sir you cannot have everything. You can have your riches and live with your unanswered questions or you can have your questions answered but give up your comfortable life.
> K.S.

So another month passed. Lord Carmichael spent his time sorting through all his father's papers. This was a job that his brother might have offered to help him with but he had decided to go off travelling.

At the back of the safe there was an old book with yellowing cuttings from a newspaper stuck inside. Lord William Carmichael almost didn't bother to look at them but as he quickly flicked the pages a young girl's face caught his eye. He read the article closely and discovered for the first time that he had a sister. A sister who had gone missing when she was just three years old and who had never been found. This news was so shocking to him. Why had he never been told?

In the weeks that followed he did lots of research but only discovered that the child, Elizabeth, had gone missing and after a massive police inquiry had never been found. He felt he could not go down to the miners until he had spoken with his brother, Matthew. He would need his brother to take over from him anyway, but Matthew was not due back from New Zealand for six months.

In the meantime he decided to visit his only other living blood relative; his father's younger brother, George. They had never been close. George was a quiet, depressed man who never seemed to laugh. He was affable enough but never opened up or seemed to contribute much in the way of conversation at family gatherings. So William felt rather ashamed when he was greeted with such a warm welcome.

"It's been such a long time; come in, come in. So kind of you to come and see me. Everything's alright I hope?"

William responded warmly. "Mostly Uncle, but I do come in need of your help, or more in need of your knowledge."

They settled down to a pleasant if plain lunch, of fresh breads, cheeses and a good red wine. "I've been going through father's papers and discovered that I had a sister. She went missing when she was three. You must know about it George. What can you tell me?"

"My dear fellow. I'd have thought you'd have known about it. She was a year younger than you, so you'd have been four when she went missing. I suppose no one discussed it much after the police case went cold. Don't you remember her at all?"

"No nothing. Just a feeling I often have that something's missing, but I put that down to mum dying."

"Well, Elizabeth was a delightful child. She was so interested in life and we all loved her. She was named after my own dear sister who went missing at a similar age. I've never got over it. Our family has certainly been cursed. My Elizabeth, your aunt, had just had a big birthday party. I remember because all the village children had come. You should've seen the mess we had to clear up afterwards, but it was great fun." George's eyes lit up as he smiled at the memory with a real warm smile that would have touched the coldest human heart.

"When your dad had a little girl he called her Elizabeth. It was a sort of tribute to our Elizabeth, but none of us ever believed that she would go missing in the same way. The similarities were uncanny. She'd just turned three as well and neither sweet lassie has ever been found."

After much talk and speculation William Carmichael returned to his mansion. He'd gone to find answers but had come back with even more questions.

The months passed and although he never failed to deliver the supplies promptly he felt he could not disappear beneath the ground without knowing what had happened to the two Elizabeths. Life however had its own plans and amidst all this pain and anguish Lord William Carmichael, eighth Earl of Christleton, fell madly and totally in love.

Melka was an artist, who painted haunting pictures of lakes that reflected strange shapes and lights. She was a tiny, fragile looking creature with pale white, silver hair and the brightest blue eyes William had ever seen. If you passed her in the street you might not have given her a second look, but if you did, her beauty seemed to seep into you. William could not believe his luck when he found that she was as enamoured of him as he was of her.

They married in the spring and Melka wore a white lace dress that glittered mystically when it caught the sun. Melka was so beautiful that William could not take his eyes from her.

In the months that followed he spent evenings with Melka in her studio; while she painted, he wrote the family history, organising and reorganising his research, to try to make sense of all that had happened. They were peaceful evenings spent in a beautiful room, lit by a silver and glass light that was shaped like a raindrop. They were happy and in love and although the life beneath the ground and the two Elizabeths were never far from his mind, William was content.

Within a year Melka gave birth to a beautiful daughter and was most insistent that the child should be called Elizabeth. William would have given Melka anything, but he stubbornly refused to have his daughter called that name. Melka could not understand it and jokingly suggested the Welsh name for Elizabeth, which was Bethan. She was surprised but happy that William agreed.

Each month William sent down supplies promptly to the miners and in between times he spent his time with Bethan. Melka disappeared for hours to do her paintings but William didn't mind as he was a most besotted father.

The years passed and Bethan grew to be a delight. Melka decided that she would give a big birthday celebration for Bethan to celebrate her third birthday. They invited all the children in the village and opened up their home. It was such a good day and there were so many presents, it just was not possible to open them all.

The next day however, William woke to his wife screaming. It took him a little while to realize what she was saying, as he had never heard her scream. "Where's my baby? Where's Bethan? Melka was hysterical and a big black cloud descended over William's heart. The curse could not be continuing.

The whole household searched, as did the police, but Bethan was nowhere to be found. Uncle George came over to see if he could help and Matthew, the doting uncle, seemed almost as wretched as William. Melka cried and cried until no more tears came and William paced the house and gardens, opening doors and looking in cupboards. Eventually he went to the secret part of the cellar, although he knew there was no way that she could get in there, because of the hidden locked, wrought iron doors.

As he sat down by the conveyor belt he noticed there was a tiny red ribbon lying there. It took him a moment to realize that it was from Bethan's favourite bear. Suddenly he breathed a sigh of relief. If Bethan was with the miners then she was alive, and they'd made sure she had her teddy. He knew what he must do and although he wanted to rush down to the mines he made himself go back to his wife. He needed to appoint her to look after the family secret and duties; then he would go and spend his life with Bethan. But gentle as his wife was, she was having none of it. Her tears stopped and she looked less worried. William felt as if she also knew that Bethan was going to be alright, but how could she?

Quickly Melka packed their belongings and Bethan's, while he went to explain to Matthew about taking over the title and duties of the Lord of the Manor. Matthew was very reluctant but agreed to do so because his brother was so sure he would find Bethan.

"Please promise me that somehow you will let me know that she's been found," Matthew said and William agreed, although he had no idea how he was to do this.

Soon they were carefully descending the narrow stone stairs that ran alongside the conveyor belt and then William banged loudly on the second thick iron door at the bottom.

"Welcome William Carmichael," greeted Kelman, who then turned and hugged Melka tightly. William registered that they knew each other as Bethan leaped into his arms.

"Daddy, daddy, granddad said you were coming, but you'd got a bit lost." At last William was reunited with his daughter and he was happy. He had a million questions but they would wait.

"Come on daddy, let me show you the lake and where we're going to live," and she tugged at his hand. As William was pulled by his excited daughter he noticed the people mostly had silver white hair, like his wife's. The cave opened up like a cathedral, with magnificent glass walls, covered with great chunks of glass. It occurred to him that these could well be diamonds. The lake was vast and beautiful, reflecting strange lights and colours and he knew this was the inspiration for his wife's paintings. All around him was a wonderful calm and beauty that took his breath away. Bethan chattered non-stop, she was so pleased to see him.

As they sat by the lake a lady came to sit with them He recognised something about her although she was a stranger. "My name is Carmel, but I used to be called Elizabeth. It's so good to have my brother here at last and of course my niece."

Bethan interrupted, "Carmel's been looking after me. She's OK. I'm going to pick up some pebbles for the next box." William kept his eyes on her at all times. There was no way he would lose her again.

As he watched his daughter, Carmel started answering his questions.

"The miners had been mining for salt for many years and the Carmichaels had lived off the profits. When the salt became too difficult to get out it was decided to close the mines, but virtually on the last day Scott Kelman found diamonds and of course took them to the fourth Lord Carmichael. The Lord was a greedy man and conned Scott to go back in the mine and then he locked him and his men in. He told them he would supply food in return for the diamonds, but he couldn't let them out as everyone would come and steal the diamonds."

"That's appalling."

"It is, but Kelman was not a stupid man. So they rationed the food and stock piled it and then they made some demands. Proper supplies would be sent down in return for diamonds and the men's wives would be collected and brought down. Also in return for the diamonds Kelman made the greedy and wicked Carmichael sign over his first born daughter and each new Lord would have to give up their child to live in the same conditions in which the miners were expected to live. Kelman thought that at least this would ensure they received good provisions in the future. Of course after the first child was delivered the others were taken because the greedy fourth Lord Carmichael could never admit to being so evil. Kelman thought that by trading his child Lord Carmichael might realize what a wicked thing he was doing, condemning people to live underground, but he never did. In fact each Lord has just followed the rules and taken the diamonds until you started to question everything.

The good thing was that the women who came down originally, realized the potential of the place and they all worked together to build a society where everyone was valued. One of the wives saw the first massive truckful of diamonds that was going to be sent up and said let's just send up a few and see if that will satisfy him. She emptied her trinket box and they filled it with the smallest diamonds they could find and the Lord thought that was wonderful. This meant the men did not have to do anymore mining, so everyone worked on making the place a wonderful place to live."

"It does look beautiful, but are you happy?"

"Oh yes. We have a wonderful life. In the light room beyond the lake there are diamonds right up to the roof of the mountain and there's a small opening to the sun. The light's reflected round and magnified. Over the years one or two walkers have found their way here but they've opted to stay. That's how we found our way to get out, but very few of us want to. We spend our time being creative. We paint, play music, write and there's plenty to do for exercise. We share all the cooking and we make beautiful things for our homes. We pay no taxes, have no money worries and there's no stealing or vandalism."

"There's one thing I don't understand. Was Melka sent out to trap me? I thought she loved me."

"And she does. She was allowed out because of her art. She wanted to mix in the art world to get other perspectives. No one's really supposed to go out but we always think of the needs of the individual and she has such talent. When she fell in love and we found out who with, no-one could believe it. We knew we could trust her but she wouldn't come back because she wouldn't leave you."

"She was distraught when Bethan went missing. Wouldn't she know it would happen? "

"She probably didn't think her dad would do that to her. Her dad's Kelman Simms. He's a descendant of Scott Kelman. She's the apple of his eye but I think he was missing her. I'm sure her distress was genuine and it wasn't a good thing to do, but we knew you'd come and she'd realize Bethan was safe and I did look after Bethan."

Bethan hearing her name rushed over to show her dad the pebbles. He ran his hand over the diamonds and hugged his daughter again.

Later as Bethan showed William the space where they would live, he found Melka and he knew they would be alright.

"How are you feeling?" she asked.

"I'm fine. I just wish I'd brought the family history I was writing, although in the greater scheme of things it doesn't matter. And I did promise that somehow I'd let Matthew know that Bethan was safe. Can we do that?"

"My dad's already done that. He's requested her unopened presents are added to next months supplies. I think Matthew will figure it out."

Melka picked up Bethan to take her for a shower in the warm waterfall. As she left she pushed a large canvass bag towards William. "Perhaps you can unpack that, while I'm out."

William unpacked all Bethan's clothes and toys and neatly put them in her cosy part of the cave. It looked quite like home. At the bottom of the bag was his research and drafts of the family history. He would have time to do it now. Then he heard ....

"So is William in here?"

William stepped out of their cave space, through the heavy handmade tapestry curtain that marked the boundary of their new home and there before him, he met his Aunt for the first time and later he told her how much George missed her.
Perhaps another Carmichael would be joining them soon.

Iona

The thick creamy envelope with the single letter H lay on the hall stand. Iona, knew what it was and who it was for. Her father would pick it up when he came down from his room. He was remarkably sprightly for a septuagenarian, but he did take much longer to get going in the morning than he used to. She had not taken off her walking boots at the door because mornings were very rushed but she had scraped them carefully before she came in so as not to leave mud everywhere.

The hilly landscape covered with tiny heathers and moss with sheep wandering all over the place was where she liked to start her day. It was her heritage and looking away from the village, her family owned the land as far as the eye could see. It had the freshest air and the most striking scenery, with mountains in the distance protecting them from the constant interruptions from mobile phones.

She tossed her almost black hair back, out of her hazel eyes as she went into the dining room to help herself to the substantial breakfast that was laid out there.

"Good morning my dear, I hope you don't mind my having some breakfast. The door was open, so I let myself in. I'm waiting for your father," Giles Wentworth said, sitting at the table with his plate piled high.

Iona put on a smile. "Would you like me to let him know you are here?"

"Oh, don't bother. He'll be down later."

'Which you very well know,' thought Iona. She went and helped herself to some breakfast and sat down opposite their aging neighbour, who in her opinion was in their family home far too often. He lived on his own and since retiring from the police force seemed to have little contact with other people and was always dropping in. Her father, a kind man, recognised when other people needed support and always made Giles welcome.

Sometimes Ramsey, her elder half brother would join her for breakfast but there were times when he missed entire days because of his fondness for whisky. He was highly sociable and great fun, but quite unreliable. Not having any interest in the land, he had studied architecture and was currently overseeing their father's barn conversion. Keith, the younger half brother managed the estate. He would be out working by this time in the morning but would try to get back for a second breakfast around ten, which he shared with their father. The whole family only got together regularly on Saturdays for breakfast and Sundays for lunch. This was expected and it made her father happy. Friends were always made welcome, so it was never a chore.

Iona sat in the magnificently sized room, with its comfortable furnishings and made polite small talk to Giles and wondered how the boys would react to father's plans.

She left Giles helping himself to another plate of food and walked briskly to her cottage on the edge of the estate. There she quickly showered and changed into her business suit, grabbed her bag and set off to work in Aberdeen. Some people felt the city was grey and bleak but it had a lively port and an international bunch of people. Iona loved the contrast of her home and her work. She had the best of both worlds.

When her father and mother were handfast and the wedding was on the horizon it is rumoured that Ramsey threw incredible behaviour tantrums and Keith retreated to his beloved animals and the outdoors. The young boys understandably resented that anyone should replace their mother, who had died suddenly. But soon they had become as charmed by her mother as her father was and when Iona was born she had been adored by her half brothers. The family were happy for a good ten years until her mother had apparently fallen in love with someone else and disappeared with him one night. She never contacted any of them again. Her mother was not spoken about because everyone knew it upset her father. Sometimes Iona felt that she could explode with the longing just to mention her mother.

Not long afterwards Aunt Tilly moved in to help out her brother with his three children. She was consistent in telling the children that they were loved by all their parents, even those who were not with them and they all found a staid, secure type of happiness.

Aunt Tilly was warm and kind and ten years older than her brother. Everyone loved her and were very sad when three months ago, she passed away in her sleep. It was a jolt for William their father, who made the trip to Aberdeen to make a new will at the law firm where Iona worked. Traditionally under Scottish law everything went to the eldest son but these were modern times and William wanted to make sure that all his children were provided for. It was his idea to convert the unused barn behind the old house into a massive modern home. There would be a large open plan area downstairs and beamed bedrooms on the upper level. William originally intended this to be Keith's living accommodation but Ramsey volunteered to take on the project. He sorted out the plans, dealt with the builders when there were problems and chose all the necessary materials. For all his wayward ways he was managing the project efficiently and with sympathy for the old building.

Keith managed all the estate business and Iona could not remember a time when he had not. Even as a child he'd been with the workers helping out. It was also Keith who loved the old house with a passion. He had ensconced himself with a comfortable study and was building a significant library of land management and history books. William knew his sons well and although they loved Iona they had hinted that she should not inherit in her own right. This was not because of a lack of love but neither of them wanted another man dealing with the estate when she married. They would always see that she had a home and of course were happy if he, their father allocated some valuables to her, perhaps the odd painting, (which in the past would also have gone to the eldest son).

Iona laughed at their old fashioned views and was well qualified to challenge them as she was a successful and sought after solicitor. She bumped into her boss Walter in the corridor of the office building as she arrived at work.

"I'll be coming down on Saturday to your place to explain your father's will to you and your brothers. I dropped it off last night. Actually I'm sure William will explain it but he wants some back up in case you all argue."

Oh, do you think I'll be allowed to attend?" Iona asked jokingly.

"I'll say I need you there to serve the tea," came the quick reply.

Breakfast on Saturday morning was as usual a relaxed affair. The family were gathered, Walter had arrived and Giles seeing the visitor's car decided to pop in and find out what was going on. Nobody mentioned discussing the will, with the hope that Giles would return to his own home, but Giles was nothing if not persistent. Eventually William gave up.

"Well Giles we are now going to discuss my will, which is a private family matter, so we'll see you later."

"Och, William, surely there's nothing private between us auld friends. Don't be daft."

But unusually William stood firm. "There are some matters that are private Giles. Please do excuse us," and he led the others into the sitting room and Giles had no choice but to leave.

Iona, Keith and Ramsey all shared a disbelieving look, as Giles slammed the door with a bad tempered muttering.

"I have seen so many families fall apart because heirs did not know the contents of the will prior to the death and I do not want this to happen to my family. If you don't like the contents of this will then argue with me about it now, honestly and openly. I've invited Walter along to explain any legal parts because I don't think Iona should be answering the family's legal questions."

"I don't see that it matters, as she won't be a main beneficiary," Ramsey stated.

"My dear Ramsey, we are no longer living in the dark ages. I have three children and I love them all totally. In the past everything was left to the oldest son, but then he had to take on all the responsibilities for the haill family and be the heritor, with responsibilities within the parish. Times have changed. Anyway this is my will and I hope you will all respect it."

William picked up the creamy thick paper. He did not read from its contents but started to tell them the gist of the contents. As he did so the envelope with the letter

H fell to the floor. He was certainly head of the household at this moment.

"I have been married twice. Both my marriages blessed me. From the first I was given my boys Ramsey and Keith and sadly their dear mother was lost to me, although I do think of her still. My second marriage gave me Iona and I think we would all agree that our lives would be the poorer without her presence. Iona's mother gave me over ten years of happiness and I have never believed that she left me for another man. Even if she had, she would have come back to you all, who were the light of her life."

The room was so quiet you could have heard the flutter of a butterfly's wings. None of these comments were expected.

"It is my belief that something terrible happened to her, but in case she is alive and comes back when I am gone, I leave to my second wife, Frances Elise Martin, Fairweather Cottage. The rent of which shall be paid to Iona until Frances either returns or is declared deceased. To my daughter, Iona, I leave Badger Cottage, where she already resides. I also leave her the right to walk anywhere on family land while it is owned by the family.

To my eldest son Ramsey, I leave the Barn conversion and five acres of land, so that he can build his architect business and also the right to walk upon the family's land whilst it is owned by them.

To my youngest son Keith I leave the old homestead and the rest of the land, to continue to manage in the excellent way he has done, these past years. With this comes the responsibility to offer a home to any family member at times of need and to act as the heritor and support the Parish as and when required."

William looked up at his family. He had expected interruptions and arguments, especially from Ramsey, but there were none. Silence followed.

Then Ramsey took a deep breath, "Why have you never said what you thought might have happened to Frances? I could never understand how if she loved us so much she could just go. I think we should try to find her."

"Well, I shall assume there are no questions about the will, so let's move on to Frances," said Walter. "Iona and I have been looking. We have copies of the police search at the time. May I Iona?"

"Of course."

"Giles said he thought he saw her leave with a man at midnight on 19 March 1989. He couldn't be absolutely sure because it was dark, but he thought it was her by the way she walked. Apparently she marched around the place in a very definite style."

"Like Iona does now," said Keith.

"But he could be mistaken, or he could be lying." Iona felt her nerves were on edge. This was what she had always longed to discuss.

"Why would he lie?" asked Ramsey.

"Because he constantly seeks attention and because he constantly sought her attention," replied William.

"Now you mention it, I remember her telling him to back off once."

Everyone turned towards Ramsey. "Why didn't you say?" asked his father.

Walter interrupted, "Just before you go down that line, let me tell you the only facts we know from the police. Frances never again used her bank accounts or her National Insurance number to get work. When she left all she had was the clothes she was wearing, stout walking boots and a good coat. Her passport was left behind. The police thoroughly searched this house and grounds and found nothing. They spoke to many of the villagers when they had their incident room at the Howff, but nobody is recorded as having seen or heard anything, although many people reported that she'd be out walking at all times of the day and night."

"Did they search Gile's place, if he was the last to see her?" asked Keith.

"If they did it's not written down here. Besides he saw her and the man from his window. She wasn't at his house. They'd have no reason to search and of course with him being in the force maybe they just took it for granted that he was not involved."

"But perhaps he was," said Iona. "Why is he so interested in this will? What does it matter to him, who inherits what? I think we should search our property again really thoroughly and if we find nothing we should find a way to search his."

"Iona, you know you can't do that. It's illegal. Even searching your own land could be dangerous if he did something and finds out we suspect him." Iona loved Walter for saying "we suspect him". He had helped her so much over the last few years.

"This is what we'll do," said Ramsey taking charge. "We'll search this house from top to bottom. Keith and I will work together and you Iona can work with Walter. When we've done that Keith and I will search our outbuildings and land and if asked we'll say we're preparing a survey to split up the land between us.

We'll think about Giles' property later. What do you think?"

William was nodding his head. "When you heard Frances telling Giles to back off, what did she actually say Ramsey?

"It's nearly twenty years ago. I can't remember. He was pestering her and she was saying something like, it's never going to happen. I just can't think."

"Think of her face, of her voice. Was she irritated or angry? Was she secretive or open? Iona suggested.

"She was speaking quietly, but I think she was angry."

"What, I'd like to know," said Keith "is if he knew her before she met father. Forgive me Iona, but I wonder if she has ever been in trouble with the police."

"That's worth checking out. Someone get the coffee on and I'll go and make a few calls. I think I know someone who could look that up for me," replied Walter.

At last Iona felt that they were getting somewhere. She had been stupid to think that nobody else cared. It was just a subject too painful to talk about.
Half an hour later Walter returned with the news that Frances had been arrested and charged with possession of marijuana when she was sixteen and the arresting officer had been Norman Carter, Giles Wentworth's boss.

"Perhaps Giles was blackmailing her to be more friendly than she wanted to be, but whatever he was up to he didn't mention that he knew her before, to anyone here or to the investigation team at the time. That is very odd. I must advise you all not to do anything to raise his suspicion and alert him. The police are going to re-open the files.

William visibly relaxed into his seat.

Much later that day both their house and Giles's house were being searched thoroughly. Inspector Agnes Rae did not like her weekend disturbed and she was brutally efficient, even if she lacked anything that passed for good manners. Giles tried pulling the old boys act about having been in the force, but he was firmly told to allow the officers to do their job. When Giles saw the thoroughness of the modern force and no weak link he was worried, but when they found the hidden door to the cellar he knew there was no way out. He confessed to arguing with Frances and said that she had fallen and died. He hadn't meant to kill her. Inspector Agnes Rae disliked liars even more than having her weekend disturbed and led him away.

In some ways it was true he hadn't meant to kill her. He'd seen her out walking that night and thought he'd waited long enough. He'd been so obsessed with her that he had been quite surprised by the level of her resistance. In the struggle his temper had exploded and he'd hit her. He could still hear the crack as her head hit the ground. Strangely as time passed he became as obsessed with her family, although in a different way.

It was a month later that the family buried Frances Elise Martin. Ramsey stood up in church and told how she had brightened their lives with laughter and kindness. Keith read out a poem Frances had written and Iona sang her mother's favourite song.

Although Iona was devastated by what had happened she was glad that her questions had been answered at last. William was sad that Frances had thought he would have held the mistakes of her youth against her, but she hadn't left them all willingly and he knew she had loved him as he had loved her.

As for Giles, he spent the last years of his life in prison; not a pleasant place for anyone but especially not for an ex-policeman.

[H means head of the family; haill means whole; handfast means engaged to be married and howff means community meeting rooms.]

The Poppy Fields

The incessant rain dribbled down the back of her neck but it could not make her feel worse than she already did. What was the purpose of standing here with all these wilting paper poppies, remembering people who had been dead for so many years? She was only here because her grandmother had wanted it.

There was a field of poppies laying on and around the cenotaph. They were cartoon poppies, just poor imitations, surrounded by lots of serious looking people and some fidgety youngsters.

She thought of poppies as they should be, dancing to the song of the wind on their delicate stems. She remembered how she had run with her boyfriend through the poppy fields, with the sun shining on their backs and how they had found such delights with the blood red poppies shielding them from passers by.

The silence was over at last. She made to go, but a woman as old as her grandmother stopped her.

"Thank you for coming and showing that you care. So few youngsters understand now, how we loved our men and how we miss them still, even though we've had another life since then."

Suddenly she understood why she should be at this service. Her grandmother had come every year to remember her love, lost in the war. Today she was standing in for her grandmother who lay in hospital recovering from an operation.

She took her poppy from her coat, kissed it gently and placed it with the other poignant poppy tributes. Then she turned to go home to her boyfriend. She understood about love.

Time to Go

The beach seemed to stretch for miles into the distance. It was wide and clean and glowed a wonderful golden colour in the fading evening light.

Ellen skipped along, just in front of her parents, chattering away.
"Robert is really pleased we've come," she called over her shoulder. "He's going to spend some time with us."

Sam and Aileen looked at each other sadly. It was almost a year to the day since their dear son had been ruthlessly mown down by a car, outside their home. Their daughter Ellen had not grieved, or cried or even once claimed to miss him. For her Robert had not left. He was with her constantly in her mind.

They had consulted the doctor, who had told them that everyone deals with the loss of loved ones in their own way. If something was too painful to deal with then we may pretend that it had not happened. Doctor Allen had told them that Ellen would let Robert go when she was ready. He had suggested that they did not make a big thing about her conversations with Robert.

The days and weeks passed and while they painfully grieved, Ellen included Robert in everything. She shared her sweets, showed him her paintings and talked to him incessantly.

"We're just going off for a paddle," she called as she stuffed her socks into the sandals and ran towards the sea.

Aileen turned towards Sam, "This has got to stop soon. Maybe we need to take her to see another doctor. Ellen can't go through life talking to Robert. People will think her strange."

Sam hugged his wife as they both stopped walking to look at their daughter, paddling in the sea. She seemed so happy. "Maybe you're right my love, but just for this week let's let her be. Next week we'll think what we have to do."

During the days they sat on the beach or paddled in the sea. They ate hot dogs and candyfloss. Aileen read books while Sam watched his daughter build sandcastles with moats and turrets.

As the weather was fine there were many other families on the beach. Abersoch had always been a favourite family place. They had come last year. Robert had played on the beach. He had even made friends with an old sheep dog from the Beach Hotel. It had spent many hours in their company; seemingly free to roam wherever it wanted. In fact the young man who owned him worked on the beach teaching people how to surf.

It should have rained on Wednesday. It should have been a dark, cold day with winds as strong as a hurricane. It was the anniversary of Robert's accident. Perversely the sun came out, as it had every day so far on their holiday and the sky was blue. Aileen and Sam had decided to make the day as normal as possible, so they set off down to the sea.

They sat in their usual spot and watched as Ellen started building a massive sandcastle. As they watched they noticed that Ellen was so engrossed with what she was doing that she had stopped chattering to Robert.

Later during the day the sheep dog from the hotel trotted over and sat beside Ellen in the middle of the sandcastle. They sat together in companionable silence. Sam went over to ask how the sandcastle was coming along.

"Robert is leaving tonight. He said it would be nice to take a walk along the sand to say goodbye. We can do that can't we dad?" asked Ellen.

"He says he has to go and that we know that he loves us and his love will stay with us. Apparently you can only stay for so long and then you have to go onwards."

Sam promised that they would walk on the beach, not knowing if his daughter was going mad or if it was just a child's way of saying good-bye. He helped to fill the moat up with water and then they stood for a moment and admired their handiwork.

After they had eaten their evening meal they all trooped down to the sea front again. It was still light but the sun was much lower in the sky. They walked peacefully along the beach; each with their own thoughts but the warmth of the day made them feel content.

Ellen said her good-byes to Robert and then she turned to her parents. "Robert knows you can't see him but he says he'll love you always and he must be going."

Aileen and Sam said, "We'll always love you too, Robert and you are always in our thoughts." The sheepdog bounded down the beach to join them and stood with them. Suddenly the light changed. It went darker and then the sun went very orange. Robert appeared fleetingly before them. He kissed his sister and blew them both kisses and then the light faded and he was gone. The sheep dog started barking into the quiet of the night.

There were no words to say. Robert had looked after Ellen as he had always done and stayed with her until she could cope on her own.

"Come on mum and dad," said Ellen, "don't be sad. Robert gave me a present." Ellen unclasped her hand and there lay a beautiful coloured shell. "If we want Robert to hear us, well he can anyway, but if we hold the shell it will help us and he will listen. Of course he can't reply but he said we'll know his reply."

Sam put his arm round Aileen and took his daughter's hand as they walked back along the wide quiet beach. The golden glow stayed with them as they retraced their footsteps. Time to go home.

The Future Calls

I lifted the flap of the tent, ducking my head and blinking my eyes in the dim light. The enclosure was draped with rich coloured materials and threads of spangled glass and crystals. The lady sitting before me shivered but did not look up. She sat as still as a statue and her silken garments with their highly embroidered patterns flowed generously to the floor. As I stood there awkwardly, the world outside seemed to retreat and a silence enfolded us.

After a few moments the lady said, "I am Catrina. We do not have long," waving her hand for me to be seated. "There is much trouble ahead." Her intense blue eyes looked directly at me. They looked full of deep concern, like a mother's caring for her child. She continued," I see a dark road with much danger lying before you, but do not despair. Within you there is the ability to see the way. You must trust your instincts and remember always that, if you feel danger then that is because there is danger to feel."

My heart went cold. I had not expected such a look into the future when I had entered the fortune-teller's tent. I had expected to be told that I would meet a tall dark stranger. I thought their unwritten code of conduct did not permit bad news. I suddenly realized that I was holding my head in my hands and when I looked up Catrina, the fortune-teller had gone.

Catrina had left quietly, without my crossing her palm with silver. Indeed she had not actually looked at my hands but I had no wish to cheat her. I delved into my bag and placed ten fifty pence pieces in a row on the desk. I had won them earlier on a side stall with a throw a hoop game. As the last coin touched the table so the noise from the fair started bursting into my mind and I got up to leave.

Outside the world was as I had left it. The ground was spongy because so many feet had trodden over the earth. There were children screaming with excitement on the rides and families having a go at winning the prizes on the stalls. Floaty pink clouds of candyfloss were walking about attached by sticks to children and the sky was punctuated with coloured balloons and streamers. The fair was crowded with happy people enjoying a not so cheap night out, but my joy at being there had diminished and I decided to go home.

Tonight I had been going out to dinner with Mark to celebrate that we had been dating for one year.

"Sorry Terri, I can't do dinner tonight. I have to meet some clients." Mark said as he came out of his bathroom this morning.

"Are you serious? It's our anniversary. Surely they could've seen you tomorrow."

"We've been through all this before. While I'm still building it up, business has to come first," Mark tugged on his shirt as he was speaking. "Anyway I'll make it up to you at the weekend."

"I know we said your work must have priority, but why on earth didn't you tell me last night? Then I could at least have done something else." I could hear that unattractive whine in my voice, which I wished wasn't there.

"Well I just didn't, so that's that."

"No it isn't. You should've told me earlier," I continued.

"O.K. well if you want the truth, I knew you'd go off on one and I didn't want to ruin the evening. We did have a lovely time didn't we?" He smiled at me with that winning smile.

I knew I had been wrong footed but by this time Mark was going out of his front door and making his way to the garage. "Don't forget to lock up when you leave," he shouted. Minutes later I heard his BMW leave.

I had gone to work feeling very down but as usual my work lifted me. I tutor in mathematics at the local university. Mathematics is such a beautiful subject. It is exact and precise. It is logical but it also has an abundance of pattern and repetitiveness that is reassuring. I love that moment when a student suddenly realizes that they have found a pattern or a method of doing a calculation. You can see the dawning of understanding in their eyes.

On my drive to work I had seen the fair. I decided that tonight I would go to the fair and enjoy wandering round, just as I had done as a child. My Gran had always taken to me the fair when it was in town. She passed away about three months ago, so tonight I would go to the fair and remember her sense of fun and her love of people. The one place she would never let me go was the fortune-teller's tent.

"That's strictly for adults," she'd say. "You have to be old enough to know that everything they tell you could apply to anyone. It's ok for a bit of fun as long as you don't take it seriously."

Naturally the one thing I always promised myself to do when I was older was go to the fortune-teller's tent. Now that I had done so I wished that I hadn't bothered. I decided to head off to my home and watch a DVD when I realized that my laptop with its integrated DVD player was round at Mark's place. So I went there first.

The house was in darkness as I inserted the key into the front door. We both had keys for each other's homes because nowadays we spent most of our time together. We had been ticking along quite happily going out a couple of times a week and then a few months ago Mark started being more serious.

"It's too early to be living together and it's quite nice to have our own homes. We don't want to rush things but let's show our commitment by spending more time together and being more a part of each other's lives." Naturally I had been in agreement. He was so dynamic and exciting and when he smiled his eyes lit up his face and you felt that all was well.

His house was quite a large three-bedroom semi. My place was a tiny little flat at the top of a big old house. It was what I called cosy and Mark called pokey, but we still had good times there.

As I entered his house I switched the light on, went into the lounge and picked up my laptop, which was stacked neatly against one wall, where I'd left it. The room seemed warm, which surprised me, as no one was home. It was then I noticed two wine glasses on the coffee table. I remember thinking that I'd washed up yesterday. Obviously I was mistaken. I was about to put down the laptop and pick up the glasses to wash, when I heard a noise from upstairs. Hugging the laptop to my chest I crept towards the bottom of the stairs.

You must trust your instincts and remember always that if you feel danger then there is danger to feel.

Is this what the fortune-teller was warning me about? Strangely I felt frightened but not in danger. Quietly I crept upstairs and paused on the landing outside the bedroom I had slept in the night before.

I heard some giggling and then I heard Mark's distinctive voice, "…here have another drop of champagne."

There is much trouble ahead. The fortune-teller had been so right. My whole life had just shattered.

I turned and crept downstairs still hugging my laptop. Like a robot, I turned out the light and put the key back in the door to close it as quietly as I could. I made my escape as efficiently as a thief in the night and it was only when I was in my car and driving away that the tears started to fall. I felt both anger and a terrible sadness at the same time.

Everyone had warned me about Mark. My mother, my friends and even one of Mark's school friends Jeremy had said, "Just make sure he doesn't hurt you. He's a bit of a lad is our Mark." I knew better than them all. He loved me. He made me happy and he was even going to let me invest in his up and coming business. I had recently inherited twenty thousand pounds from my beloved Gran. I had been going to use it as a deposit on a little house, but Mark told me he had a business opportunity that I really couldn't miss. Anyway eventually I would move in with him full time, once the business had really taken off. I wanted to move in immediately but Mark was more sensible. He said we should take our time. All the papers were drawn up and we were due to go to the solicitor next week, for me to sign and become an investor in his business. I had been such a fool. No wonder he did not want to rush.

I found myself driving out to the country. There was nothing about. The roads were empty and it started raining. That suited my frame of mind. I travelled along narrower and narrower roads, without any idea of where I was going. My mind whizzed round all the times spent with Mark and the future that I thought we would spend together. Everything had changed with the sound of that giggle.

Suddenly I realized that I was travelling far too fast. I was coming up to a blind bend and there were black and white warning arrows and red triangle signs at the side of the road. The image of ten fifty pence pieces set out in a line flashed before my eyes. I slammed on my brakes so hard that the car jerked violently to a halt. Luckily nothing was following. I sat there for a few moments gathering my thoughts and gradually realized that there was an amber glow ahead, intermittently flashing.

I stuck on my hazards and walked round the corner. There in front of me was a mangled car embedded in the side of a tree. The couple in the car had missed the turning into the narrow entrance to a farm and hit the tree. The rain was now pouring down in torrents as I rushed over to the car. I pulled out my mobile phone and found it had a signal. Although I did not know the location I managed to give the emergency services the name of the farm, which was signposted clearly. The occupants of the car were both still alive but unconscious and I decided to leave them where they were. It seemed to me that the car was unlikely to explode with so much rain pouring down. This was probably insecure logic but luckily it worked out that way.

It seemed like hours passed, standing in the pouring rain and in pitch-blackness except for the amber glow, which lit up the scene one minute and quickly hid it again in the next. I didn't try to switch off the indicator. I wasn't sure how. There was complete silence except the sound of my squelching feet as I moved from one side of the car to the other checking the pulses of the two injured youngsters. I should have felt alone and scared but I knew that I could have easily joined this tangled mess of metal and if I had not stopped, there would have been no hope for any of us. Eventually sirens blasted through the night accompanied by blue flashing lights and a policeman shouted at me to stand back. The couple were taken to hospital.

The following day a strange thing happened when I went to see how they were getting on. I was looking through the window in the ward where the girl lay and her mother was sitting by her bed. If I hadn't known better I would have sworn that the mother looked like Catrina who had told my fortune. She glanced my way and our eyes met. They were intense blue eyes and it seemed a flash of recognition passed between us. Obviously it was just a coincidence. As a mathematician, logically, I know how frequently coincidences occur and we have all seen people who look like other people. Strange though!

Mark was very surprised when I told him that I would not be seeing him anymore or investing in his business. I never did explain why. Let him work it out. At least it will dent his ego. His friend Jeremy has called a couple of times since he saw me at the hospital. He works there in the pathology laboratory. He is tall, with dark hair and has never said,"I told you so."

Now as I sit in my little newly bought cottage and think over the events on that night, it occurs to me how Catrina's words rang true. *Within you there is the ability to see the way.* Sometimes as I curl up on the sofa in the happiness of my new home I shudder at the thought of what my life might have been like if I hadn't gone to the fair? I don't dwell on it for long though. I have a lovely home and a lovely job and thanks to Catrina, the future calls.

Missing

Melissa was running through a dark forest of legs, keeping her round blue eyes on the thin bare legs in front of her that she knew she mustn't lose. If there was a pause in this race, she would lean her head backwards and try to catch a glimpse of the sky. She had learned long ago not to make a fuss as it was seldom tolerated and she could end up with a sharp clip to her head or indeed to any exposed area.

Sometimes when her mother's skirt was long enough she was allowed to hold on to the edge of it, which made life a lot easier, but today's skirt was short and tight with nothing to grab hold of.

Once she had completely lost her mother but the aftermath to that episode was not to be repeated. The sweetness of her mother's smile when she was returned was transformed into a mask of hatred that she would never forget and her ears had hurt with withering comments that accompanied the slapping.

It was during one of the brief periods of respite, when they were waiting to cross the road that Melissa first noticed the lady in the brown coat. There was nothing remarkable about her except she was smiling at Melissa's level while she picked up something from the ground. It was not just a mouth smile. It was a crinkly eyes smile and Melissa couldn't help herself smiling back.

The moment was over. Her mother was crossing the road and she had to keep up. She could see the legs and almost reach out to them. Then her mother disappeared through a heavy wooden door, which Melissa ran through just before it shut.

Soon she was sitting outside the ladies changing room in an overlarge chair. Her feet were parallel to the floor and she stayed where she had been plonked down. While her mother tried on a number of outfits Melissa noticed the lady in the brown coat again. She was standing near the exit and she was beckoning to Melissa. Once again she smiled and Melissa, who had been on her own for quite some time, clambered down from the chair and made her way over to the lady.

The brown coat held out her hand for Melissa and said they would go home by car. As soon as they were through the swing doors she picked Melissa up and held her closely. Melissa felt safe and wanted for the first time in her life.

"Are we going to my home?" she asked.
"No" the lady replied, "but it will become your home."

The lady settled Melissa into the car and sat her on the brown coat, because she didn't have a car seat. Then they sped away up the motorway, stopping briefly for supplies and a teddy bear. Soon they had disappeared.

As they travelled, large floury snowflakes began to fall. Melissa thought it was wonderful and by the time they arrived at the little cottage everything looked magical, covered with a blanket of snow.

Melissa's mother emerged from the changing rooms to find her daughter missing. She went over to the cashier's desk and paid for her purchases before she raised the alarm. But by then Melissa was long gone.

Sacked

Simon decided to enter the building confidently with the keys he had surreptitiously copied. He had been made redundant two weeks ago on 17 October 2008. He knew that he was taking a risk. They may have changed the security code but he gambled that they hadn't. It was he who had always instigated the code changes and he'd always had such a battle to get agreement with Ben, his boss.

As he'd expected the building was completely empty. A month ago there would have been a night receptionist but with the cutbacks Old Tom had to go. When he punched in the number the alarm did not go off and he realized that now he could implement his plan.

His footsteps echoed hollowly on the shiny marble floor and he darted into the security room, rewound the tape and turned off the master switch to the security system. Entering the lift it seemed to be clanking loudly but Simon realized this was probably due to his heightened perceptions in an empty building. After what seemed an age the lift the doors opened and he went towards his old office.

"Well Mr Denton, I wasn't expecting to see you here."

Simon's heart almost stopped but he recognised Old Tom's voice. He took a deep breath to calm himself.

"Hello Tom. I could say the same. You were made redundant the week before me."

"Ah but that was then. This job's been my whole life. I like the peace and quiet, so they let me come back, although I don't get paid." He chuckled.

"That's very good of you Tom. I want to say how sorry I was that I had to be the one to end your employment. I hope you know I didn't want to. When they did it to me I realized that I should have fought for your job and for the others. I am sorry."

"Oh well, it's done now. So what *are* you doing here?"

"I've just come back for a few of my things. My pen that my wife gave me and the mug that I got for Father's day. You're welcome to come with me to see I don't take anything else."

"Oh goodness me, you go and find your things. As if I wouldn't trust you, Mr Denton, after all the years we've worked together. No I'll carry on with my rounds. I know you'll not be up to mischief." He chuckled again.

Simon thought the chuckle was a little strange but he must now decide what to do. He'd been seen. Should he change his plans or just go for it?

He entered his old office and noticed immediately how girly it was. There were potted plants around the room and a pink desk tidy. "Stupid bitch," he thought. Ben had given that young Samantha his job, for much less pay of course. She knew the basics but she wasn't in his league and she'd obviously lost the argument about changing the entrance code. Well she'd have her work cut out on Monday.

It was obvious he was in trouble anyway so he switched on the computer. Carefully he disabled the firewall and all the anti-virus software. As the computer was part of the network and he'd logged in using the admin code, this would affect all the computers in the company. He reached into his pocket for the pen drive he'd loaded with a program he'd been working on this week.

"So Mr Denton, have you found your pen and mug?"

"Goodness Tom, where did you come from? I didn't hear you creep up on me."

"Oh old Tom doesn't creep. I expect you were concentrating. It's a shame you can't send a virus thingy round all the computers, isn't it? That'd serve the buggers right. What are you doing, downloading your address book?"

Simon felt a bit unnerved that Tom was so near the mark with what he'd been doing, but decided to bluff it out. "Yes Tom, I don't want to lose my contacts. It's so good you understand. He stuck the pen drive in the USB port and opened up the program.

"How's that lovely wife of yours and young Charlie?" Tom asked.

"Well she's still lovely but if you must know she chucked me out when I lost my job. Said I was a loser. I still go round every few days 'cos she let's me see Charlie, but I have to ring first. Can you believe that a man has to make an appointment to see his own son?"

"That must be hard for you. I have a friend who might be able to help. Would you like to meet him?"

Simon launched his program and set the start time for 9 am Monday 3 November. As he unplugged the pen drive a different voice spoke.

"Hi Tom, did you want me to do my party trick?" A man stood behind Tom. He was wearing what seemed to be an old track suit.

"Where the hell did you come from?" Simon asked, his heart beating faster and his skin seeming to burn.

"I hang out with Tom here sometimes. He thought you might like a quick view into what your wife's up to. Watch the screen."

Simon knew something was terribly wrong. It was just possible that Ben would have allowed Tom to come back without pay, but there was no way he would have permitted Tom to bring his friends round. Nevertheless Simon's eyes strayed to the computer screen. After a few seconds he saw his wife, beautiful, naked and extremely energetic with another man. She arched her body backwards and he saw that the other man was Ben. So that's why she used his redundancy as an excuse to chuck him out.

"What have you done, bugged my house?" he demanded.

"Not exactly." The stranger replied.

"Looks like you've been used," said Tom. "Ben got you to downsize the staff. Made you do all the dirty work while he was taking liberties with your wife and then sacked you." Was there a tiny smirk behind his eyes Simon wondered? He couldn't really blame Tom if there was.

The screen went blank. Simon had seen far more than he wanted to see. He knew there was no way back. She'd never been as enthusiastic with him.

"It's a shame you can't burn down the building. But I expect the jammy old so and so has the place insured for more than it's worth, so it probably wouldn't work." Tom's words hung in the air.

Simon knew that Ben didn't believe in insurance. Oh he had public liability and employee insurances because he'd had to, but he'd never bothered with the building insurance.

"I suppose you stay here all night? He commented to Tom and his friend.

"No not tonight, we're off to a party. Well we'll leave you to it. Make sure you lock up when you leave."

"OK Tom, have a good party."

"Oh we intend to." Tom replied.

Left on his own Simon sat down at his old desk and switched off the computer. In his mind he could see the passionate couple engrossed in each other and his heart ached for all that had never been and would never be. There was complete silence in the building but it offered no comfort. Suddenly he noticed a small lighter on the desk, which was very odd as it was a no smoking office. The idea that Ben would lose everything played on his mind. Of course torching the place rather negated all his hard work, writing that program, but it would be more difficult for Ben to start the business again. He picked up the lighter and returned to the security room, where he disabled the fire alarm.

"TOM" he shouted over and over. The words echoed in the empty reception, but there was no reply. He had no wish to kill anybody.

Alone in the building he threw paper down, found some cans in the store room with flame warnings on and sprinkled the liquid liberally around. At first the fire flickered and looked rather pathetic and Simon thought he was going to fail at yet another task. Then it took hold and he realized he needed to get out. He ran to the front door but it was locked. His key wouldn't open it. The temperature was rising. He ran over to the windows, pulled up the blind. He was ready to chuck a chair through the glass but the sight outside made him stop. There was Tom, his friend and twenty or so other slightly strange looking people and they were dancing. He banged on the window but it wouldn't break. Then they came up to the window and peered through. It was a terrifying sight. They pulled faces and laughed. He heard a cackle and a scream of delight. They were enjoying his terror. Simon clasped his hand over his mouth to keep the fumes out. He thought he was going to faint. He watched as Tom flattened himself against the glass and emerge on his side of the window. Simon couldn't breathe. He thought his lungs would burst.

"Your wife's right you know. You are a loser. Did you really think I'd forgive you after you took my whole world and shattered it? I'm surprised you didn't read about my suicide in the local paper. There was nothing left for me to live for when you'd sacked me. Now I've these new friends and I'm really enjoying watching you suffer. Ben used you to do his dirty work and now I have and you'll always have that image in your head of your wife. Your trouble is you let people lead you. You're weak. You don't think for yourself and nothing is ever your fault." There was so much hatred in his voice that Simon knew this was the end.

"So now you're going to kill me."

"Oh no. That's not my style. I've had my fun and my revenge. I expect you'll kill yourself. Or should I say I expect you have killed yourself." Tom laughed and morphed back through the window.

Simon knew he had only minutes left. Suddenly he realized how much he wanted to live. He could change. His mother had always said how bright he was. He must think. There must be a way out. Helplessly he ran to the fire doors but the bars were jammed. He was coughing and choking. His eyes stung with the heat. Then he remembered. In the delivery bay there was a back entrance; an up an over door that opened from the inside, which was normally alarmed and electronically locked. Not only could he get to the delivery area because the security system was switched off, but he'd be able to open the door for the same reason. From somewhere in his memory came the thought that smoke rises, so he bent down and on all fours; he found he could see and move better. Once inside the delivery room, he shut the door to the main building. It was less smoky and he gasped a few breaths. Then he ran over to the delivery door and threw it upwards. Soon he was outside in the night air. He could feel the heat from the building as he ran away, but he could also feel the cold from the night air. How refreshing it was. Now he knew how precious life was and how much he wanted to live it. Perhaps his wife no longer loved him but his son did. Tomorrow he probably would be arrested, but if not he would look for work. After all people with IT skills were always in demand.

Slowly he began to rebuild his life but every now and again Simon would hear Tom's words and see the faces at the window. But Tom had gone long ago to another world.

Lady in Waiting

"She's not my mum," Tom told his teacher in a loud voice. "She just married my dad."

I wanted the floor to open up and swallow me, but Mrs. Stone smiled at Tom and calmly said, "Well that's nice for you; it means you have twice as many people to love you."

Tom muttered something under his breath as Mrs. Stone explained that Tom had ripped his trousers during playtime, which was why he was wearing his P.E. shorts.

We left the school in silence, side by side, but not holding hands. Tom put up with my presence but he made sure that I knew he did not like it. It hadn't always been like that. When I first met his dad we had all got on very well. The three of us would go out to the park or for a walk in the country and we always had a lovely time. Sometimes we would take a picnic or we would take some bread and feed the ducks.

"Andrew is coming to tea tomorrow. Mum said that I could always have my friends round," Tom announced in a defiant voice.

I took a deep breath. The last thing I must do was to lose my temper. "Your friends are always welcome Tom, but you must ask first, because we might have something else planned. As it happens, we are free tomorrow, so it'll be all right. Now what would you like me to make for your tea?"

"My mum never asked. She always knew what I liked." Tom replied.

I put the key in the lock of the front door and once inside, headed for the kitchen. What I needed was a cup of tea. I carried through a tray with orange squash and chocolate cake for Tom and then I sat down beside him and put my feet up.

"How much longer is it before the baby comes?" Tom asked as we sat watching one of his favourite programmes on television.

"I can't be absolutely sure but it should be about a month," I replied.

"What if we don't like the baby?" he asked. "Nobody in my class is having a baby, you know. Fancy having a baby sister when you are eight!"

"Tom, the baby is going to need us all to love her. You see the baby will be completely helpless and will need to be fed and changed and cuddled. I'm sure some of the children in your class will be very jealous that you'll have a baby sister."

I was in the kitchen making the evening meal when Martin came home from work. "Hi Sarah," he called to me as he made his way through to say hello to Tom. I laid the table and served the meal and we all sat down together. Tom was a different child again when his dad was about. He was well behaved and polite and usually quite happy, so I was not expecting the flood of tears that followed.

"Aunty Sarah was very cross with me today Dad, because I ripped my trousers at school," he blurted out.

Martin shot me a surprised look, but said quietly, "I expect she was cross that the trousers will cost a lot to replace. I don't expect that she was really cross with you."

He put his arm around Tom and the crying stopped. I looked across at Tom and he looked away. At least he looked embarrassed, so I decided not to say anything.

Tom tolerated me reading him a bedtime story but turned his face away as I bent to kiss him goodnight. How much longer would this go on for? I wondered. I felt fat and tired and would have liked to burst into tears, but what good would that do?

After school the next day Tom and Andrew came out of school giggling.

"Thank you for letting me come to tea," Andrew said as he saw me. "You do some of the best teas ever."

Tom only said, "Hello," but at least he was smiling.

"What are you going to call the baby?" Andrew asked as the boys were eating their tea. "Some parents choose the most dreadful names."

"I have no idea. Why don't you two go and think of some?" I replied.

They rushed off to the other room, taking a pencil and paper with them. I cleared the table and made Martin his meal. It was much easier to look after Tom when Andrew was about. He was such a friendly child and Tom was so much happier when he wasn't on his own with me.

We were sitting eating our meal when the boys came back with their list of names.

"I think you should call it Jessica," said Andrew enthusiastically.

"Don't call the baby IT, Andrew, she is a person." Tom replied.

"Quite right," I said, "but that is a nice name Andrew."
Did you have any ideas Tom?"

"No," he said and left the room.

"He did have an idea," Andrew said, "he thought of
Samantha. The first two letters are from your name
Aunt Sarah, the next two are from yours Uncle Martin
and the 'TH' from Thomas, is in there as well. He is
really clever isn't he? Without waiting for a reply he
bounced out of the room to rejoin Tom.

"Well I certainly would never have thought of that," said
Martin and we both laughed.

It had been a much nicer day and when I read Tom his
bedtime story he let me give him a good night kiss. I
was about to leave when a little voice said," Will you
love the baby?"

"Yes Tom. I hope we all will," I replied.

"But not all mothers love their children."

"I know I will, but I love you too you know. You're very
special. You don't have to give birth to someone to love
them. I love your dad and he certainly isn't my son."
I hoped I was reassuring him. It was so important that
he knew that I really did care, but his next question
really threw me.

"Why doesn't my mum love me? She never comes to
see me," he stated.

I paused not knowing quite what to say, but knew I
must say something.

"Your mum does love you. She writes every week.
Your mum and dad tried to live together but they just

couldn't get on. Then she fell in love with Alan, who as you know lives in Wales. Because his job takes him all over the world, your mum thought you'd be better to stay with your dad, so you could stay in one place and go to one school. I think she must love you very much to make such a sacrifice. Don't you?"

"Maybe," Tom replied.

"Your mum never forgets to write. Whatever else she is doing she lets you know that you're always in her thoughts. Sometimes when we love someone we don't say it in words; we show it by what we do. Her way of showing you she loves you is by writing. It can be very hard to actually say, I love you," I said.

"I know." Tom replied. ""Goodnight Aunty Sarah.

The baby arrived three weeks later. She was warm and wonderful and very noisy. Martin brought Tom to the hospital and he sat next to me and gingerly held the baby. He was totally besotted from the moment that she grabbed hold of his finger and would not let go.

"Oh yuck, she's a bit damp," Tom said, but he was laughing and did not want to hand her over.

Finally Martin said, "Well my love we must go. Tom and I are putting the finishing touches to the nursery. Bye for now."

"But what are you going to call her? She must have a name," Tom asked.

"We liked your choice of Samantha." I replied. Tom grinned and they left the hospital happy.

When I came home from hospital Tom gave Samantha his Teddy.

"Won't you miss him?" I asked

"No. I want to give Samantha something precious, so she'll know that I love her and I know you'll help her look after him 'cos you look after us all."

I knew then that Tom and I had come over a hurdle and although there would be more hurdles in the future we would all find a way through.

End of an Era

"Well that's thirty five years of teaching over! All that paperwork and stress and now's my time for a bit of relaxation." Bob eased himself into the large armchair and kicked off his shoes into the middle of the room.

"Yes dear," Carol said in a thin voice as she looked at the errant shoes in the centre of her spotless sitting room. "Tonight you can certainly relax and later we'll sit down and work out the rota." She poured him a beer and left the room to see to dinner.

Meanwhile Bob was puzzling over the word rota. What could it mean? Ah well, Carol's thinking was often beyond his understanding, so he sipped his beer happily contemplating the extra golf he'd be playing and the hours he would spend enjoying the pleasures of the 19th hole.

"This is a very nice meal dear," he remembered to say. All these years of marriage had taught him to say the right words or he'd learned you ended up having to cook for yourself. Carol half inclined her head acknowledging the meaningless and perfunctory compliment.

"Now tomorrow, after you've picked up the vegetables from the market, you can pop into mum's because she needs a door handle fixed. You might as well take your suit to the cleaners and then we can pack it away clean. I can't see when you'll be wearing it again."

"Oh you usually do all that. I was hoping to get in a game of golf," Bob's voice whined in a very unpleasing way.

"So let's just get this straight. You're going to have time off because you've retired and I'm going to carry on waiting on you hand and foot for the rest of my ... "

"Oh I wasn't saying that."

"Besides it's YOUR mother who needs help. It'll make her day you popping in."
Bob knew the argument was lost and carried on eating his meal.

"You can stick your clubs in the car and pop into the club on your way back and I'll have your dinner ready for you when you get in. Well at least by seven."

"That means I'll be out all day," Bob moaned.

"Oh for goodness sake, it won't do you any harm; a few little errands and then a bit of exercise."

"I just thought if I got a game of golf in early we could spend some time together in the afternoon. Oh well, I suppose we could do something together the day after tomorrow."

"Well that'd be lovely dear, but mum's got an appointment at the hospital for her hearing and it'll take you a while. The parking's so bad you'll have to get there at least half an hour early and whatever time you arrive at mum's, it'll take an hour to get out of the house."

"I can't take her to the hospital. I've never done it. I won't know where to go and anyway medical things are best done by a woman. You'll have to go. She won't be wanting me along." Bob drew himself up in his chair. This was not how he had intended to spend his days.

Carol gave him *the look*. It should have warned him. "I don't think you're listening very carefully to me, dear."

The voice held that little edge. "She's not having anything *female* done to her. She's having her hearing checked. Now you're not telling me that a man of your intellect, a retired teacher no less, can't manage to take his own mother for a hearing test, are you?"

"But you'd be much better at it than me, Carol. And you've been before. You know the doctors and the right questions to ask."

"Precisely."

"What do you mean precisely?"

"I mean that since you explained to me that there was no way your mother was going in a home, I've spent most of my week looking after her. There's the hairdresser on Monday and shopping on Tuesday. The chiropodist is every other Thursday and usually there's two or three medical appointments a month. Sometimes they take all day. I've done them all for the last four years, without complaint. Now it's your turn."

"But..."

"There's no "but" about it. You'll have plenty of time and it'll keep you out of mischief."

"I just thought we might be going out together more and enjoying ourselves, now that I've retired." Bob paused in his speech as Carol went to answer the phone.

"Yes, Mrs Harvey. I'll be there promptly at 9. I'm so looking forward to it."

Carol couldn't quite look Bob in the eye when she came back into the room. She took a deep breath and blurted out," I'm starting work at St Jude's Hospice

Charity shop in the High Street tomorrow. It's my turn to go out to work now."

It was a happy solution for Carol. They had been married for a *very* long time. She picked up his shoes from where they had been discarded and dropped them neatly on his lap.

Over Time

Bethan loved this time of day. The building was quiet and no-one would interrupt her work with inane questions or unimportant messages. She settled into her computer chair and hit the paperwork that needed to be shifted. The sun gave an orange tinge to the office and she felt happy. When eight o'clock came she packed everything away, set the alarm and left the empty building.

One day followed another much the same and although Bethan worked long hours she was always home by eight thirty, which her husband had decreed was the latest she should stay at work. Bethan knew she was neglecting him but if you wanted to get on in this world you had to put in the effort. Her fashion jewellery business was just really taking off. She'd started it with the money her Gran had left her, much to Martin's displeasure. He thought she wouldn't make a go of it but she was proving him wrong and he'd had other ideas how the inheritance could be used. He was annoyed that Bethan stood firm but she had seen how quickly he could make money disappear.

It was on a Thursday evening in June that her life began to change. She opened her front door and Martin's strong, sharp aftershave assaulted Bethan as usual.

"Have you seen the local paper?

"Well hardly," she replied, "I've just come through the door. What does it say that's so important?"

"There's been a murder at Sandchester. That's just down the road from your work."

"How awful." Bethan kicked off her shoes and went to open the fridge door. She was gasping for a cup of tea. Taking the milk out and placing it next to the kettle, she was half listening to her husband.

"The murdered woman was thirty eight, just two years younger than you. She was walking her dog and when she didn't come home her husband went out to look for her and she'd been stabbed."

"Mmmm, that's not very nice," Bethan said as she poured the boiling water onto the teabags.

"Not very nice! A woman your age is murdered just round the corner from your work and you say it's not very nice. What I want to know is do you lock your office when the other staff have gone home?"

"Martin, the woman was out walking her dog. She probably came across some drug pushers and they killed her to keep her quiet."

"In other words, no. You leave your door wide open for anyone to just walk in. I want you to promise me that you will lock the premises when the last of your staff leaves. In fact I insist that you do and I may come and check."

Bethan raised her eyes to the ceiling and agreed. There were times when it was just easier to give in.

For the following three weeks she locked herself in the office when staying late. It was still her favourite time of day. Once or twice she heard noises in the empty building and had to fight the urge to go and investigate. She even went home a bit early on a couple of occasions. Her lovely solitude had been tarnished but not yet ruined.

One evening as she sat in her office listening for noises, she heard a key in the lock. Her heart started pumping louder.

"It's only me," called her cleaner, Sarah. "I left my mobile phone. What're you still doing here? You should've gone home hours ago."

Taking a calming breath Bethan replied, "Just a few things to do."

"Oh there's always things to do. What's with this locking yourself in? You never used to?"

"Martin insists. He's worried about my safety since that woman was murdered in Sandchester."

"Well I see his point, especially if the building was locked all day but you could look at it another way; if the murderer got into the building during the day you would actually have locked yourself in with him. At least if the door's unlocked you'd be able to get out quickly. Kick him hard and run"

"Well thanks for that little gem Sarah."

As soon as Sarah left, Bethan picked up her things and followed. She was not in the mood for work.

"They've still not found the murderer," Martin greeted her when she got home.

"The police have said that they've been unable to work out what the motive was. The woman had no enemies and never took her purse out when walking her dog. She was well known and well liked in the area. I hope you're still locking yourself in when you're on your own."

"Yes Martin" Bethan replied but she no longer had an appetite to work late in the office. For several weeks she lugged work home and worked on the dining room table and the next morning she lugged it all back to the office. Martin, who was always cross when she worked late, was now even more bad tempered with having their home cluttered with paperwork. It seemed nothing she could do was right. Eventually Bethan had to admit to herself that everything was getting on top of her.

"This is ridiculous," she thought to herself. "There is no reason why someone should want to murder me. I've allowed that poor woman's misfortune to wreck my life but it can't go on." That night she decided to stay late and get the paperwork done. She checked the building from top to bottom when everyone went home and put her key in the lock. Then in her head she heard, "you would actually have locked yourself in with the murderer". She turned the key. "At least if the door's unlocked you'd be able to get out quickly," came into her head. Bethan took a deep breath, unlocked the door and went to her office.

Stoically she worked for two hours. A floorboard creaked but Bethan refused to let herself investigate. She must not give in to this neurotic fear. She'd been safe before the murder. She was still safe. Feeling pleased that she'd cleared some work she took her cup into the kitchen.

It was dark and shadowy in the kitchen. She could smell bleach. Sarah had obviously been bleaching the teaspoons or the mugs again. Sarah was addicted to bleach, but there was another familiar sharp smell. Suddenly she felt very uneasy. As she bent over the sink large hands grabbed her throat and pressed hard. The world went cold and white but she knew she had to fight. With one hand she dug her nails into a hand round her throat and with her other she reached for a large mug containing some spoons on the draining board. She thrust the mug over her head at her attacker. The spoons clattered to the floor and some liquid went onto her hand. There was a scream and the throttling hands loosened their grip. A strong smell of ammonia reached Bethan as she turned ready to run. Her attacker was cradling his face and screaming in pain.

Bethan paused for a second in shock and then realizing there was still danger ran to the door. She dashed out of the unlocked door and didn't stop running until she reached the safety of the petrol station on the corner of the street.

She knew she had been lucky. She had left the front door open because of Sarah's words. The bleach on the teaspoons had given her time to free herself. Her husband had been taken to hospital and was now in police custody. One day he would be free again but by then they would be divorced. He needed to know that he would not inherit her Gran's money if she died. Only then would she feel safe.

Sands of Time

It was ten years ago that my world was upended and I learned that my mother and new boyfriend had done the unthinkable. Now I am sitting on a deserted beach at Abersoch, just five minutes away from mother's house. It is five-thirty in the morning and there is absolutely no-one about. The sea is lapping gently against the flat golden sand and the sun's rays are low in the sky. These are my sands; a place and a time, to think and find the evasive answers to those difficult questions.

Today is the day when I will visit my mother for the first time since leaving home. We will break our years of silence and see what is left of our damaged relationship. Whatever she saw in Ben, my boyfriend at that time, they're still together. My mind is in conflict because a part of me feels we are thinking human beings, in control of what we do and a daughter's boyfriend is off limits but I also feel you should love your mother. It's expected. Ben is unimportant now. Time is slipping by but the beach is still mainly deserted. At the far end is a person with a dog. They are so far in the distance I cannot see if it is a man or a woman. The sun is a little higher and brighter and is sparkling on the sea. Near the edge of the sea a gull is strutting on the flat wet sand, leaving tiny delicate footprints like handmade lace.

Mother had me when she was sixteen. When I met Ben she was still young but she'd never shown any interest in my boyfriends before. She'd always seemed rather amused by them but I suppose Ben was different. He was so energetic and quite a bit older than the few young men I'd bought home. There was nothing in my life that gave me an inkling of what lay ahead.

We'd all been having a pleasant Sunday, reading newspapers, eating Sunday lunch, watching motor racing, when the telephone shrilled into our day. My best friend Shoana was having a crisis of the boyfriend variety and so I rushed off to see her.

I was back home within five hours to find my world was completely shattered. In hindsight I suppose it was not very polite to invite Ben over and then go out, but it was an emergency and you don't expect the people you love to betray you within five hours? It was unbelievable! Their attempts to fight their uncontrollable passion seemed very superficial to me. It took me about ten minutes to pack and I haven't been home since.

Shoana and I had gone travelling for six months. We'd visited many European cities and then spent a few months in New Zealand. When we had the opportunity we worked on farms or helped out at hotels. As we didn't have work permits we were paid by free bed and food, which helped to eek out our meagre funds.

When it was time to come back to England we rented a place together and rebuilt our lives. I finished my teaching degree and went to work in a large secondary school. I soon discovered a real empathy with young people, who need help with their behaviour and have low self esteem. I now work part-time and although the work is incredibly hard, I love it. It is so rewarding.

Shoana trained as a nurse and is working in a hospital. Nowadays she is married to a lovely man called Malcolm and they have a young son.

I walk slowly along the beach, dreading the next few hours, but enjoying the feel of sand between my toes and the beauty of the morning. There is a warm gentle breeze but it is time to get going. The beach is beginning to populate with early morning dog walkers

and people bringing down sailing dinghies and boards.
I run back to the hotel and quietly shower and change
into a flowing gypsy style skirt and plain blouse. I do
not want to look as if I have made any effort for this
meeting, although I actually have spent ages choosing
something that I feel good in. I spend a few minutes
applying some eye shadow and pale lipstick and brush
my hair until it shines. Quietly I slip out of the hotel
room and walk to my old home a few streets away.

"Oh I can't believe you're here," Mother greets me as
she pulls me into a bear hug. "Come in, come in."

Ben stands back, but says, "Nice to see you, Lucy.
You're looking well." He looks me up and down
appreciatively, and gazes into my eyes, so I walk past
him not acknowledging his look, but with a polite,
"Morning".

Mother offers me coffee and we sit down in the living
room. The room is the same as when I left. It's not
been decorated or changed in any way. As ten years
have passed, it's now looking tired. Mother reflects the
room. Her make up is the same as it used to be but
now seems too heavy. Her eyes do not hold the wicked
sparkle of a decade ago. They look sad. Ben looks
bored.

"We're so glad you've come home," mother says.

"I'm just visiting."

"Well what've you been up to? Tell us your news."

I explain about my job and how much I love my work,
but omit to say where I'm working. I tell them both
about my travels with Shoana and how much fun we
had exploring new places and meeting new people.

"What about yourselves? What's your news?" I ask.

"Oh, we've been on a few good holidays," Ben replies, but mother does not look happy or confirm the information.

"I'm still working for the same firm," mother adds "and I do a little job at the local restaurant."

"Goodness mother, why are you doing that? Surely you shouldn't be doing two jobs." I ask before I can help myself.

"Ben was made redundant and hasn't been able to find another job." Mother's voice was unnaturally calm and Ben looks away. Something is wrong here, but I feel I have stayed long enough for a first visit and a part of me isn't sure that I want to be involved.

"I will be in touch again very soon mum, but I have plans for the rest of the day and need to get going. It's good to see you."

"Before you go, I'll just give you a picture of your cousin's wedding. It's just upstairs. I won't be a minute."

As soon as she leaves the room Ben whispers.

"Lucy, meet me later. You're looking so good."

"Meet me at the Swan at twelve," I quickly reply, as mother is coming down the stairs.

I say good-bye to them both and make my way back to the hotel.

At midday I am sitting at a table in the Swan. Ben swaggers in and sits down with a big grin on his face. "What would you like to drink?" he asks.

I look up to the man standing behind him. Max, my dear husband of just over a year, is just returning with our drinks.

"No, what would you like to drink? Max asks. "Do introduce us darling."

"Ben, I would like you to meet Max, my husband. Max I would like you to meet Ben, who I've told you about."

Ben shakes Max's hand enthusiastically but then remembers an urgent appointment. Although he smiles at us both he is obviously squirming inside. I am surprised that my insipid bit of revenge gives no real pleasure. Seeing the two men side by side reinforces what I already know. There really is no comparison. Max is also a good looking man. I love every minute I spend with him. He had known to pretend to be asleep this morning when I returned to the hotel after my early morning walk, sensing that I needed time to think. He hadn't pressed when I'd said I wanted to visit my mother on my own or even when I'd told him about this meeting; he'd waited until I suggested he should come with me.

I know now that Ben really is unimportant, but I've known it since I met Max. Ben is obviously living off my mother and probably has done so for several years. He's not making mother happy and I suddenly feel a rush of sympathy for her.

Later that evening as the sun is sinking in the sky, Max and I walk along the sand. There are other couples meandering along the beach and one or two families are still playing games. I stoop and pick up a handful of sand and let the grains trickle through my fingers like an egg timer showing the passing of time. So much time has passed since I left this place. So much in my life has changed.

"How're you feeling?" Max asks. "Has the ten year break helped to heal the wounds or do you still feel raw?"

I turn and look at my lovely husband. "I feel good. I'm so glad we came. My mum is going to need some emotional support soon. Ben's still looking around and one day he'll find someone who can pay his bills more lavishly. If it's alright with you I'd like to invite her over to meet her granddaughter. It will give her a new lease of life."

"That's why I love you, Lucy," Max says as he gives me a hug. "You've a generous heart. We'll not wait too long before we have your mum over. I'd love to meet her. Now let's get back to our daughter. I expect Shoana and Malcolm will be ready for a rest."

A golden glow spans the entire beach as we walk slowly back to the hotel. Both of us happy to return home now, knowing we'll be back soon.

The Busy Street

The street was crowded with Christmas shoppers. Everyone was rushing around. I just merged into the throng and slowly made my way along Oxford Street. I won't pretend I wasn't nervous, but I didn't think THEY would be looking for me, at least not yet.

"Stop that woman! Stop that woman!" the security guard shouted. Not even thinking about what I was doing I stuck my foot out and the woman went flying and then crashed down with a thud onto the pavement. Melissa, my best friend at school had taught me that move during netball practice. It makes me laugh when commentators on telly go on about footballers; they should see us girls in the inter-schools netball matches.

"You bitch," the woman screamed at me and started to move towards me but the large security man stepped in between us.

"You need to come too," he called over his shoulder as he led her back into the shop and I felt I had no choice but to follow.

In spite of what I was doing that day usually I was well behaved (apart from the viscous netball matches), but I really didn't want to be around when the police arrived. I wasn't in school uniform and although I didn't really look like an adult, perhaps I could've passed for someone who'd recently left school. As a precaution I'd stuck a clip in my hair and pulled it up because it made me look a bit older and I didn't want to get caught.

First they took the woman into a back room and then another security guard asked me my name. I had to think quickly.

"Jessica Brown."

"Shouldn't you be in school?"

"INSET day."

The security guard looked at me kindly. "OK, if you say so, but just a word of advice. The police will be here in about ten minutes and they'll need your statement. Whatever you do, don't lie to them because they'll find out."

I drew myself up to my full (well almost) five feet "What'd she do? The woman your mate was chasing."

"She pulled a knife on a cashier. The cashier was very frightened. That's why it's so important that you tell the truth for your statement."

Later a female police office came to interview me. When she asked my name I replied, "Sally Turner." The security guy winked at me and he never let on that I'd lied.

Of course I was in trouble at home. Mum and dad found out I'd been up to London. They thought I'd gone to shop but they didn't find out what I'd really been up to. The boy I'd been on my way to meet was on the telly that night. (He turned out to be 38!) Apparently he'd done some things he shouldn't have done to a girl of twelve, like me. I've erased everything from my computer, so nobody will know I'd arranged to meet him. I've learned my lesson though and I did help stop a thief, so the parents haven't been too bad.

Living on the Edge

It's funny really that everyone is looking for me, but they don't know who I am. Yet I'm here everyday, not hiding away in a safe house.

Skiing is magnificent. When you're at the top of a mountain you can watch the other skiers like little ants skittering about in trails; tiny and insignificant people. The mountains are exactly the opposite; they are dominant, imposing and almost claustrophobic, walling you in. It's a world of transition and strangers so I don't stand out here. My parents ran a skiing shop and so I've skied since I was a bairn and I'm good. Truth be told, I'm good at everything, particularly my job.

It was a shame that Albert had to die. He seemed a decent man; a man with principles. I suppose it would be nice to have principles. When I slipped that poison into his glass he hadn't a clue. Like I said before when I turn my hand to something I get it right. The best part of course was arranging for that particular poison so that everyone, including Albert, would think the Russians had done it.

It was quite risky working in that laboratory for so long. I could have slipped up and blown my cover, but living on the edge is what I love and because I sell my many skills to the highest bidder it can be *so* lucrative.

Yesterday I skied with the ants. I did three black runs and I refrained from taking anyone out, because I kill for a living, not for fun. I bobbed up and down on the chair lifts and nodded and smiled appropriately at all the little happy ants. I even drunk gluvine with a bunch of tourists in the evening but today I'm going off-piste. The challenge of untouched snow is lovely. There's a silence in the mountains that brings such peace. It's like I have total control.

I wouldn't miss the treat of today for anything and tomorrow I get paid.

I snap on my skis and set off with a swish, as the skis slice through the virgin snow. The scene before me is indescribable and there is not a single person anywhere. This is a time for thoughts, without distractions. When the war breaks, as it surely will, with everything my employer is doing, I wonder if it will still be so untouched here.

Suddenly I get a flashback - the glint of glass, hidden in the barman's hands as he'd served my drink last night, shoots through my mind. I realize with irony that I am dead by the same method I'd used to kill Albert, just as the cramps start to grasp in my stomach. I bet they didn't use a sophisticated poison like I did. I crumple down into the pure, soft snow. There is not a single person anywhere ....and I was going to be paid tomorrow.

Bad Timing

I don't know how old I was when the light dawned but I remember the occasion. Jess and I were sitting side by side at the mirror and we were playing about with mum's make up.

"Don't you think it odd that I've got dark hair and you're so blonde?" she asked.

"What's even odder is that I'm the *only* one in the family who's blonde," I replied without thinking and then I realized that what I'd just said was the absolute truth.

"That's why mum's make up makes you look so ghostly. It's too strong." Jess continued in her usually chatty way, completely unaware of the thunder in my head.

I expect I continued the conversation, but while I sat there I scrutinised our faces. She had a soft cherub face, with the family look of an English rose, whilst my face was sculptured and angular. Our eyes were blue, but my blue eyes were a stronger brighter colour. The other difference I noticed was our fingers. I had long thin fingers, which were really useful for playing the piano, the passion of my life. Jess's fingers were shorter and chubbier.

I spent the next few days thinking about each family member in turn, trying to find just one that I was like, but there wasn't one. When I cornered dad as he was gardening and asked him if I was adopted, there was that instance of panic in his eyes that told me I had hit the nail on the head.

"You're our daughter in every meaningful sense of the word. You're very special to us and we were always

going to tell you but, we didn't want to spoil anything."
He pulled me to him and gave me one of those bear
hugs of his.

Life went on as if nothing had changed but inside I
knew it had. I continued to play the piano at every
opportunity. The dining room was my sanctuary. The
piano dominated the room and I sat for hours
ploughing my way through both classical pieces and
popular tunes. Mrs Wentworth came once a week to
teach me. They were free piano lessons because Mrs
Wentworth had entered me for a music competition
when I was six and surprisingly I'd won.

My music became an integral part of family life. I
played at everyone's birthday and as I became more
proficient I played at weddings and parties and even at
Aunt Agatha's funeral.

My mood dictated the music I played. When I was in
trouble I played loud, angry music and when I was
happy I'd play bright quick pieces. It became a family
joke, but I never minded because I was always allowed
to go and play on my dear old piano.

Mrs Wentworth told me when I was very young, that I
had a good ear for a tune, but bad timing. She made
up funny phrases that fitted the rhythm for many tunes.
Finally after a lot of hard work I improved and
eventually passed all my music exams.

Now I am waiting outside the office of Miss Davina
Soammes. She is a top solicitor in London and has
reluctantly agreed to see me. Dad and I took a long
time to trace her and he offered to come with me but I
wanted to do this myself. My palms are sweating and
I'm sure my smart trousers suit must look tatty after my
journey.

"Come in, Stephanie," Davina says in a cool professional voice. She is wearing heels as sharp as javelins.

"Thank you for agreeing to see me." I sit opposite her and start to scrutinise her face. It is a smooth face with no lines and her make up is immaculate. I can't help but compare her face to mum's, which is full of lines. Mum's eyes have deep fans that spread from the outer corner and fall off her cheeks.

"I'm not quite sure what you want from me but we have half an hour and we won't be interrupted."

There is no warmth or welcome. I am not the child she has thought about every day. I take a deep breath and ask all those questions I'd always wondered about.

"I want to know why you gave me away, what hereditary illnesses run in the family, what family talents run in the family, if I have any brothers or sisters and anything else that might be relevant to my life, like who is my birth father?"

"Well that shouldn't take half an hour," she smiled at me for the first time and I realized she had a sense of humour.

"I just want some honest answers."

"OK and then you'll tell me if you have been treated well and if you have a good life."

I agree.

"Right, there are no hereditary illnesses that I know of. There are no siblings. I gave you away because I would be an appalling mother, so I made sure there were no more mistakes."

Inside I flinch, but I don't show this. She has set the ground rules and I will play her game.

She continues, "When I found out I was pregnant I was about to be made a partner in the firm. I'm sorry but you were just bad timing. I'm afraid your father was bad timing too. He was over keen so I dumped him. There are no particular talents in the family, but we've all done well."

"Who is my father?"

"I really can't say. It wouldn't be fair to go crashing into his life as you have into mine. I don't want to be unkind. I live in a world where you have to work long hours and not have a complicated personal profile. I tried very hard to make sure that you were adopted by a really good family, who would give you everything you need. Have they?"

There is no pause for my reply.

"If ever you're in trouble I do want you to call, but let's not keep in touch otherwise. It'll just get complicated," are her departing words as she gently propels me out of the office.

Although I cry all the way home, I also realize how lucky I am to be adopted. Mum and dad both meet me at the station and hug me as if I had been away on a safari for a year. No-one mentions the red eyes.

The days pass and I realize I am still the happy person I always was and of course I have my music.

Mrs Wentworth calls and invites to her home for Sunday tea and I suspect she is going to tell me she is retiring. I will certainly miss her incessant challenges to my skills and her incredible knowledge.

When I arrive she asks if I will play the piano for her and her guest. He is a thin pale man, and I don't pay him any attention. I choose Beethoven's, "Moonlight Sonata," and sit down at the piano. The notes flow through my fingers and I am lost to this world.

At the end of the piece, both congratulate me and then the thin pale man plays a piece of music that is so beautiful I want to cry. As he plays I notice his long thin fingers and then his hair colour. My heart starts to thud in my chest as I realize his face is thin and angular, like mine. I stand up shakily and go to look at his eyes. He senses my presence by his side and looks directly at me with strong blue piercing eyes and the music stops.

"Who are you?" I ask bluntly.

"I know this'll be a shock, but I'm your father. When Mrs Wentworth told me you'd been to see Davina, I thought it was time I introduced myself."

"You wanted to meet me?"

"Always. Always. When Davina gave you away there was nothing I could do, so I paid for your lessons and made it look like you'd won free lessons. You'd been adopted. I could do nothing, so I gave you the only thing I could, the opportunity to play music. It is the only talent I have."

He is not my father. He is a stranger and I don't want to hug him and yet there is this love of music which we share.

"Play some more," I say and the awkwardness passes.

Later, after we've had tea I tell this musical father how I've always had bad timing and how hard Mrs Wentworth has had to work to help me.

"Me too," he replies, "but we get it right in the end."

Sometimes these days when I play at a family do, my musical dad comes too. We even play duets. As our fingers run over the keys, like skis over snow, I imagine what our reflection would look like in a mirror. Two bowed blonde heads, both engrossed in our playing, in perfect tune and time.

Life begins

Bob had agreed to see the interfering old busy body because he could not seem to shake her off. Persistent phone calls had worn him down. He let her in promptly when the doorbell rang and showed her into the front room, which was immaculate.

"Now, spell out exactly what it is you want and then leave me to get on with my life." Bob didn't see any reason to be polite to this intruder.

"Well, my name is Sharon and this is just a visit to see if we in Social Services can support you in any way. As I said on the phone, your daughter asked us to call. She obviously wants to make sure that you're looked after properly."

"Well Sharon, let me tell you she doesn't want to see me looked after properly to the degree where it will involve her in coming to visit. However if you would kindly arrange to put me in a home she'll be happy to take on the proceeds of the house."

"Oh Bob, I'm sure it's not like that. Sometimes when we've just lost someone, we can feel the whole world is against us."

Bob shuddered at this sanctimonious young woman who apparently knew his daughter after one phone call, better than he did after a lifetime of her "aspirations".

"O.K. Let's start from a different angle. I am sixty eight. I walk about three to five miles a day. The house is reasonably clean and I can cook a decent meal. I know how to work a washing machine. So what support would you think I need?"

Sharon looked around the immaculate room and began to wonder why she was here. Really it was not normal practice to visit on the say so of a daughter but the woman had been so persistent about how her father was losing his mind, eventually Sharon had given in and said she'd visit.

"Well you might like a home help to come in and do a bit of housework or shopping."

"No."

"If someone was coming in a few times a week at least they could keep an eye out to see you were keeping well."

"Tell me, young lady would you like some nosey busybody checking up on you?"

"Well..."

"Precisely! Now are we finished?"

Sharon stood up and brushed an imaginary spec of dust off her skirt. "Thank you for seeing me. When we get a referral we do try to follow it up but I'll reassure your daughter that you're fine."

When the door closed behind Sharon he breathed a sigh of relief. He did miss Vera, his wife, of course, but she had always organised him and told him what to do.

He opened the kitchen door. "Come on boy, time for our walk." He slipped the lead on Bertie's collar and the black labrador's tail wagged vigorously.

Bob had worked out a good survival strategy. He'd picked out Bertie from the Rescue Centre. Bertie was excellent company and not a young chap, so quite happy to take his time on a walk. The two of them trundled the mile and a half or so across the fields to The White Swan, where Bob had his lunch. There was always a friend or two in the pub and they sat a while and put the world to rights. Then it was back across the fields before it was dark. Mavis from next door had put him on to a very good cleaner, Ethel, who came in three times a week and did any jobs needing doing.

He spent his evenings painting in his new studio (the back bedroom). He didn't have to pack anything away, anymore. It was lovely to spread out and he had canvasses everywhere.

Bob went and opened Vera's jewellery box. "Thank you Vera," he said as he snapped the empty box shut. He didn't feel at all guilty because over the years he had scrimped and saved to buy most of it. His daughter really thought he'd lost all her mother's jewellery. He could have told her of course, but why should he? The jeweller had thought it all very good quality and the amount of money he'd given Bob, well it should see him out in the lifestyle to which he was becoming accustomed.

Secrets

The smile was fixed securely to his face. He had checked in the bathroom mirror. There could be no slip up. His wife must never know. The pain inside, scrunched up his stomach and his eyes felt as if they had been both been punched by a skilled heavyweight boxer. Lack of sleep had made him desperate, tetchy and withdrawn, but somehow he must act normally.

Adam drew a deep breath before he left the sanctuary of the bathroom. He grabbed his case from the landing, ran downstairs and shouted,

"Sorry love. Must dash. Be back around seven," kissing his wife fleetingly on the cheek as he left the house. The door slammed shut behind him.

Oh how it hurt to be rejected by someone. It had been so many years since he had been pushed away. His obsession had started at evening class. She had been younger, not pretty, but striking in a rather obvious way. Her lightened hair was clipped back with a glittering slide and she wore too much make up for his liking, but it had not mattered! Nothing had mattered. He had wanted her.

She had slipped him a note on the second evening. DRINK AFTERWADS? From that moment he had been hers. He would have left his comfortable home that had taken years of hard work to build up and he would have left his dear, almost grown up, family.
Adam had almost declared his feelings. After weeks of hurried meals and little gifts she had pushed him away.

"Why Adam, you naughty boy! You're married! What sort of girl do you think I am?"

The irony of her use of the word girl escaped him, for she was the wrong side of forty. It was then he begun to see her coyness, understood the subtle hints for jewellery had actually been demands, that the little loans would actually never be repaid. Like a blinding light he realized that she had used him and that now his time was over, so why did he still want her so much?

The ache grew and grew and came like waves on the seashore, again and again, but he fought back. He tried to focus on his wife and to want her again.

In the twenty-two years that had been their marriage, his wife, his best friend had helped him through any crisis that had come their way, but he could not share this pain with her. Adam thought that perhaps he should leave her anyway. If he could feel so much for another woman, then what chance did his marriage have. Then selfishly he thought that if he could not be with his new love, if she did not want him in any case, what was the point of leaving his home and disrupting his family.

The house was warm and welcoming as he entered from work. His wife had cooked his favourite meal and subconsciously he noticed how well she looked. It seemed very perverse to him that she should be thriving when he was hurting so much.

The next day, he was not sure why, instead of making his way to the office, he went and sat in one of the booths in the college cafeteria. He was quietly nursing a mug of frothy coffee and feeling not a little sorry for himself, when the voices of two women talking in the next booth jarred into his private world.

"You have to pick the older married ones or the very lonely....... They are so flattered by the attention.........

then you need reasons why you desperately need money."

"But don't they ever guess that you are taking them for a ride?"

"No, they're so arrogant that they think you really find them interesting and then you can drop hints about how those earrings would look nice, if only you could afford it...."

Adam recognised the voice and sank lower into his seat in case he should be seen. The woman he was so besotted with had really taken him for a fool. She had used him in a cold cynical way. She had manipulated his mind so that he could not think straight and worst of all she was boasting about her tactics to her companion.

When he went home that night his wife had not returned from work. He started chopping onions and tomatoes and preparing the evening meal. Later as he sat across from her at the table he looked and saw the attractive woman he had first loved. She was still good looking, slim and well turned out. He listened as she told him some amusing anecdote of her day and managed to laugh.

Adam's wife knew the moment he had returned to her. She noted when he had looked and actually had seen her again. She recognised that the preoccupied air had gone and that tonight he had really listened. Her weeks of swimming, dieting and buying new clothes had not been in vain. The advice from her friends, not to confront him had been worthwhile.

Tomorrow she would decide whether she would forgive him but tonight she would enjoy the victory of a campaign well run.

Property Deal

"The cottage we are about to view is at least two hundred years old and oozes character and class. There are two living rooms downstairs in addition to the kitchen and bathroom facilities. There is also a small study, which is referred to in the particulars as a library. Shall we go in?" Michael enquired as he opened the panelled wooden front door.

"Well that's what we're here for isn't it Simon?" Abigail Egbertson said as she thrust her way into the first of the living rooms.

Simon followed his wife quietly behind as he replied. "Yes, Abigail."

Michael raised his eyebrows imperceptibly and entered the room last. "You will see that the fireplace is a particularly dominant feature of the room, with its heavy wooden beamed mantle piece." He kept his voice calm and friendly.

"I can see with my own eyes what the fireplace is like, young man and I can tell you it's nothing like as nice as ours at home. Wouldn't you agree Simon?"

"Well, perhaps this one has a little more age to it," Simon said tentatively, but on seeing the thunderous look that frequently erupted on his wife's face he quickly added, "although ours is somewhat more dramatic." Secretly he thought theirs was gaudy and hideous, but he gave himself a pat on the back for his extreme diplomacy! His wife marched on through to the kitchen.

"The kitchen is fitted with an Aga Oven, which also heats the house. It is oil-fired, very efficient and suits a country cottage well," Michael stated.

"Well that would have to go. It is so old fashioned. We'd need a new kitchen anyway," Abigail boomed as she looked disdainfully at the terracotta floor tiles.

Simon witnessed Michael suppress a wince, as he added, "The kitchen was designed by 'The Chef's Delight Company' who are considered the best in the area. Most people can't afford them, but everyone has different tastes, don't they?"

"Well it doesn't *delight* me and it will have to go. You think it's horrid, don't you Simon?" Abigail smiled at him coyly.

"Absolutely," he said out loud. "Not," he said to himself. It really was not an argument he was going to win. He did not look Michael Stanley in the eyes as he followed through to the 'library'.

"Goodness me! How can this be described as a study let alone a library?" asked Abigail to no one in particular. "My under the stairs cupboard is bigger than this."

"This is a very compact room, but it has sufficient space for a good sized desk and as you can see the walls are lined with book cases. The removal of these would be one option to make the room larger," Michael said in a pleasant voice.

Simon popped his head round the door. There was no point in going in and indeed he could see everything from the doorway. He refrained from saying anything and went through to the other living room.

"Ah, that's where you've got to," Abigail said a moment later as she marched into the room. "Well this is very ordinary, isn't it dear?"

Simon looked around the room, which housed a well-polished piano and lovely dark wooden table with four chairs.

"There's a pleasant view out of the window. What a beautiful garden!" he replied.

"Yes there is a classic cottage garden. You'll find that there's an abundance of flowers and quite a few vegetables and fruit bushes being grown. The owners have agreed that they'll be leaving all the plants," Michael informed his clients.

Abigail peered through the window as if she could not see the view from the other side of the room. She sniffed.

"What an abominable mess. Now our garden is neat and tidy. It has a huge lawn and a regular border all the way round. It will take a lot of work for you Simon to get this one sorted."

"Indeed dear."

"Please do view the bedrooms and bathrooms upstairs." Michael said as he took them into the small hallway. "I will wait for you down here."

At the top of the stairs Simon addressed his wife, "You don't seem to like this place dear. Are we wasting our time?"

"Don't be ridiculous, you fool. It has great potential. We will make an offer, but considerably lower than the asking price. Let's just check out these rooms."

When the upstairs tour was finished Abigail thrust Simon into the main bathroom.

"OK now this is what we are going to do. You are going to go down and make an offer of £300,000."

"But that's £50,000 lower than the asking price. There is no way the owner will accept that."

Abigail paused and gave Simon one of her looks, "You will point out all the work that has to be done. Now don't hang about and don't be bullied."

"My dear I really don't think …," Simon started.

"Oh for goodness sake, I'll do it."

Abigail thumped down the stairs like a tramping elephant, to be greeted by Michael just closing his mobile phone. He opened his mouth to speak but before the words were out Abigail had started.

"Now there is an awful lot of work to be done. That dreadful kitchen has to be ripped out and replaced, the so called study needs to be refurbished and the fireplace and chimney need to be removed and that will involve a lot of building work. Now we are interested in buying the place but not at the preposterous price it is advertised…"

"Excuse me." Michael tried to intercede.

"Please don't interrupt," glared Abigail, "I find that so rude. Now where was I? Oh yes, we are prepared to offer £300,000. A serious and much more realistic price I feel."

Simon decided to be fascinated with the design on the stained glass window nestled at one side of the front door.

"What I was trying to say, Mrs Egbertson, is that the owner has just phoned our offices and taken the cottage off the market. I was on the phone to my colleague as you came downstairs."

"Well what an infernal waste of time! Come on Simon," Abigail called as she slammed out of the front door.

"Thank you for your time," Simon muttered to Michael as he followed Abigail.

Michael locked up carefully and checked that Mr and Mrs Egbertson's car was no longer in sight. Then he stepped into the garden next door and kissed his pretty wife who was digging up some weeds.

"I've just been very naughty," he said, with a grin on his face that lit up his eyes. "Did you say that lunch was ready?"

Agneta

Agneta parked her car after the long journey. She was attending a Christian retreat for teachers in Birmingham and felt hot and tired.

"Welcome," greeted Emily as she entered the wide front doors of the old house. The hallway was impressive, with rich polished banisters and heavy embossed wallpaper.

"Please do go through. Everyone's having a cup of tea."

Agneta went through into a very large room where there were lots of settees and coffee tables and a general hum of polite chatter.

"I didn't want to come. My head sent me. She reckons I need a rest. What I actually need is a weekend without all the schoolwork I have to do," a woman, she later found out was called Elizabeth, was saying.

"I expect these retreats are being offered so they can prove that they take this work-life balance issue seriously. There's been a lot of senior teachers and heads going off with stress and of course the youngsters just leave," her companion replied.

Nobody paid Agneta any attention so she made her way over to the long dining table and helped herself to a cup of tea. Then she looked over the tea cup to carefully assess if there were any friendly looking faces. She had not made up her mind when Emily appeared in the door way and clapped her hands.

"Now that everyone's here I need to take your photographs individually, so that I can make up your passes. You'll need these for meal times and for re-entering the premises if you go out. Could I have some volunteers?"

Several obliging people went over to have their photograph taken and when Agneta had finished her tea, she lined up too.

An hour later everyone picked up their pass and photograph and were asked to stick the two together. This caused quite a bit of amusement amongst the guests, who thought that "do your own" security passes, probably defeated the point of having them. Agneta found her pass but there was no photograph.

Did Emily make a little sigh or was it her imagination? She stood patiently while Emily took another photograph.

"I'll just check it this time." Emily pressed a couple of buttons on the camera but the photograph was not there. She tried again but no image appeared. "I'll use the camera on my phone," she said. "This one must be broken." Emily took a photograph using a modern slim line pink phone, but when she looked she could not find the image.

"It's new and I'm still working how to use it," she explained. "I tell you what I'll just write camera broken and sign your pass. That'll be fine." But although Emily was polite and reassuring, there was a puzzled look in her eyes.

Everyone was meeting back in the lounge at six. By that time they had to have thought what was their greatest personal achievement in the last five years. They were not allowed to include anything about work. In the meantime they were free to explore the village, the church next door, wander around the extensive gardens or go to their rooms for a rest.

Agneta walked to the church by herself. What was her greatest achievement? It couldn't be her marriage because Doug had left after six weeks. Apparently he'd fallen in love with her best friend at their wedding. It was something that neither of them had wanted. As the hurt and betrayal started to flood back Agneta made herself think of something else. There was no point in crying any more tears. She had put all her energies into her work at school but they weren't allowed to mention that. What could she use?

She knelt down in the quiet church and prayed. Suddenly the door opened and in stumbled Elizabeth and her companion.

"Oh it's freezing in here."

"Shhh Elizabeth, someone's praying."

"Oh it's only that quiet one from the group, Sam. You have to watch them you know. There's nothing much here, let's see if we can find a café."

The church returned to quiet and although Agneta did not have the answer she sought she felt calmer.

At six promptly everyone was gathered. Giles Gillingham was running the session and he was smart and efficient.

"The purpose of this weekend is to relax and to spend some time finding your priorities again. Sometimes we lose our way when we work as intensively as you all do. So now we're going to think about what we've achieved outside our working environment."

The sofas had been roughly put in a circle and Agneta began to feel very tense as each member of the course started to tell what they had achieved. Then it was

Agneta's turn. She said the first thing that came into her head.

"I've learned that I can survive, whatever life throws at me."

"Would you like to give us an example? Giles asked.

"No, Giles, I don't think I would."

"And that's absolutely fine. We're not here to put any pressure on anyone. Gordon, what about you?"

At the end of the session Giles summed up. "Absolutely everyone here has been successful in achieving something significant outside of their work and has recognised it. Tomorrow we are going to look at what we want from our lives in the next five years and we'll consider both our work and our non-working lives."

"Dinner is now served in the dining room," said Emily.

The dining room was set out with tables of four and was wood panelled from floor to ceiling. Agneta sat down at an empty table and within seconds had been joined by Elizabeth and her companion Sam. Gordon, a rather shy young man, came into the room and looked a little lost. Agneta knew that feeling well and called over, "There's a spare seat here, if you're looking."

Elizabeth raised her eyebrows, but Gordon's look of relief was worth it.

The meal was served and it was delicious. Once they had started eating, Elizabeth said," Agneta, what did you mean by, "whatever life throws at you?" Do tell us because it's good to talk."

"It's kind of you to ask but let's just enjoy our meal."

But Elizabeth was persistent. "The thing is, we all go through hard times and when you tell other people it's much better than bottling it up."

"Maybe she doesn't want to talk," suggested Gordon.

"These are wonderful potatoes," said Sam trying to change the subject.

"Of course she wants to talk," continued Elizabeth.

"O.K. Liz," said Agneta. I was just talking generally. You know the type of thing. Someone says something like, "you have to watch the quiet ones," in a rather unkind way. At one time that might have upset me, but as I grow older I realize that I can choose to consider if I value that person's opinion or not. If I don't then I don't accept the comment and it doesn't upset me."

Sam's mouth fell open.

"Actually my name is Elizabeth, if you don't mind," came the unfazed response.

"What happens if you do value the person's opinion? asked Gordon.

"Well if someone is being unkind, you have to think why. If they're making a comment you don't like, are they trying to be helpful? If they are, then I suppose you have to consider what they say seriously."

Giles walked over to their table. "Is everyone alright?"

"Oh yes," said Elizabeth, "We're having an interesting philosophical discussion."

"That's good to hear, Liz," and he moved to the next table.

That night it started to rain heavily with it beating down so loudly it was hard to sleep. Each bedroom had a large bed and comfortable chairs and a table. Agneta picked up her book and decided to read herself to sleep. Then thunder banged its drum and lightning lit the room through the curtains.

Agneta heard a banging on someone's door. She went and peeked out and saw that Sam was knocking on Elizabeth's door, on the other side of the corridor. The door opened and Agneta heard Elizabeth say, "Oh go back to bed and don't be such a baby." The door slammed shut.

Agneta opened her door wider, "I'm just having a cup of tea, if you'd like to join me."

Sam came in and they settled down to sit out the storm, with steaming hot cups of tea and biscuits that had been provided.

"Elizabeth's right. I'm a coward. I've always been scared of storms. My mum went to hospital in the middle of a storm and never came back. Logically I know the storm had nothing to do with it but it doesn't help."

"Well it sounds to me as if you're halfway to dealing with it. Rationally you know the storm's not the problem, so now you've just got to find strategies to help you cope with the fear."

"That's easier said than done."

"Is it helping that we're sitting having a drink?"

"Yes, it's much better than hiding under the bed covers."

"So maybe that should be your next strategy when you're on your own. Get up, wrap up in a snug dressing gown and make a cup of tea. You could watch a film or listen to music to distract you. Perhaps it won't help but it's worth a try.

The storm blew itself out about three in the morning and Sam went back to her room. When the alarm went off at seven Agneta reset it for 8.15 and decided to miss breakfast. She ate the last couple of biscuits and downed a cup of tea after her shower and was punctual for the first session, which started promptly at nine.

"Life can just drift if we don't have goals. It actually doesn't matter that much whether the goals are achieved and it's certainly alright to change them whenever we feel like it, but it's an idea to have a plan. In five years time I hope to be married and perhaps have a child. I'd also like to be running my own consultancy firm rather than working for someone else. So who would like to start us of about where they'd like to be?"

"I'd like to be married with children as well," said Gordon.

"Some chance," was whispered from somewhere in the room. Whether Gordon heard or not was unclear.

Giles moved the conversation on, "and what about at work?"

"Well, I've thought quite hard about this and if I had children I wouldn't want to work any longer hours than I do already, but if I hadn't I suppose I'd go for promotion."

"What a thoughtful answer and it actually illustrates a point I'd like to make. What we do in our non-work lives affects what we do at work. Gordon is recognising that children take a lot of time so he wouldn't want to extend himself at work. He could still make progress, specialize and challenge himself."

"Well I'm just the opposite. I want promotion and in my non- work life I want to buy a bigger home with a large garden," chipped in Elizabeth.

"Those two ideas fit together well. If you earn more money you'll be able to afford a bigger house. Obviously you don't struggle with the job you do or you wouldn't want to take on more responsibility, so thank you for your thoughts, Liz."

Fleetingly Elizabeth realized that she didn't want more responsibility but she dismissed this thought because it would interfere with her plans.

"Agneta what about you?"

"I'm really happy in the job I do, Giles, and in my non-work life I'd like to write a book of poetry."

"No ambition, some people," Liz muttered to Sam.

Giles smiled. "Well Agneta, in your position you have nothing to prove"

"I'm happy where I am. It's a village school and the years have their highpoints and routines."

"Thanks Agneta."

Later as they had lunch Agneta heard Emily talking to Giles. "She really scares me you know. I suppose you're paid to be pleasant to everyone but I took her photograph several times on two cameras and there was no image. It really freaked me out. I just feel she must be in touch with the devil if she doesn't have an image. Well have you met anyone without one? It's like vampires don't reflect in mirrors."

"Emily that's fiction. There's probably a very simple explanation. You and I have worked together a lot and you're always imagining things. Give the girl a break. Perhaps you pressed the wrong button and deleted the pictures or maybe the battery ran out."

"Well we'll see. I shall take a group photograph tomorrow and that'll prove it one way or another. Pure evil is what I think though."

For a Christian retreat there was a lot of very unholy, unkind behaviour going on. Agneta, tried to apply her own logic to what she'd just heard. She was not close to Emily so she did not need to take on board the rubbish she had just spoken. Except was it rubbish?

The afternoon was their own and they had to meet again at 6pm with an idea of something they were going to do for themselves that they would enjoy. Agneta went out to the church. It was silent, peaceful and the sunshine shone through the stained glass windows. She sat down and prayed. As she prayed she realized that almost everything that she had prayed for, since the break up of her marriage, had been granted. That she'd have the strength to carry on; that little Tracy at school would recover from Leukaemia; that the vandalism problem at school would be resolved and suddenly she was worried. What if somehow she had made a pact with the devil when her heart had been full of anger? Now she prayed really hard that somehow God would let her know that she wasn't evil.

Her concentration was so great that she didn't notice Gordon slip into the back of the church. He sat down at the back, so as not to disturb her and saw a wonderful light shine down on her. It could have been the sunlight shining through the stained glass, but Gordon didn't think it was. Somehow he'd walked in on a very special moment.

When she stood up and noticed Gordon at the back of the church she made her way towards him.

"I don't suppose you'd like to go out sometime," he asked as they walked back to the gardens.

"I'm not ready to date anyone, Gordon." And she told him how her husband had left her so quickly after their marriage to go and live with her best friend.

"The worst part is that for a time my heart was so full of hate, that perhaps it has made me not a very good person. Do you think it could have made me evil?"

They walked through the formal gardens to the wild area that sheltered a large pond.

"I don't think someone who was evil would be worrying about it. No you hated their behaviour and you obviously were extremely hurt. Do you hate them now?"

Agneta thought about it, "No, I don't particularly want to see them, but no, I don't hate them." As she spoke she knew that it was the truth. "Thank you Gordon."

They walked round the pond, enjoying the beauties before them. The reeds swayed in the wind and the wild flowers waved pale straggly stems all around them.

He thought about telling her how the light in the church had danced around her, but stopped himself. She would think him mad.

When they walked back to the lounge Emily was sitting with Sam and Elizabeth.

"So what have you two been up to? asked Elizabeth.

"We've been walking round the pond at the end of the gardens, discussing all the new friends we've made. Perhaps we should all exchange e-mail addresses" suggested Agneta.

"Oh er yes, what a good idea," replied Elizabeth.

Later Giles asked them to share their ideas of one thing they were going to do for themselves.

When it came to Agneta's turn, she said, "I'm going to write a formal letter to my governors to thank them for suggesting this retreat. It's done me the world of good."

Giles beamed. He liked praise as much as the next person and if the retreat had been a success, part of that was down to him. Gordon was also happy. He knew that he had helped Agneta today. Elizabeth didn't particularly like the woman, but couldn't credit that she was evil, as Emily had just suggested. In fact she remembered that Agneta had been much kinder to Sam last night than she'd been.

When the session ended the group stood up to go to the dining room.

"No, wait everyone," Emily instructed. "Group photo. Now if you all could stand close together. That's right. Smile." She took far more photos than usual and as they sat down to dinner she pressed the buttons on her camera.

At dinner she pushed her camera towards Giles. "Look, everyone else is clear but there's just a white space where she was standing." Look, see if I'm right."

He ignored the camera and took another mouthful of potato. "My dear Emily, do you know what Agneta means?"

"No."

"It means pure. I don't think she's evil at all. Why don't you get on with your meal?"

At the end of the meal, Giles picked up the camera, "Look Emily, there she is. You must have been mistaken."

Two weeks later Emily downloaded the photographs she'd taken and she was very pleased with them. They were really clear and showed that everyone was enjoying themselves. They would brighten up the Retreat's monthly newsletter.

It was only Giles who noticed that Agneta's image wasn't in the photograph, but he wasn't worried. She was a bright lady and would work out how to create images once she realized the power within her. It had taken him about three years and if needs be, he'd help her.

Birthday

How can a man of fifty-five still be excited by birthdays? The tension had been rising for about three weeks. What would he get for his birthday? Was it going to be a surprise or would I like some ideas?

Believe me I have ideas!

I smash the margarine onto the sugar with feeling and batter it until it loses its shape. I chuck in the flour and eggs and whiz them with *my* two month old birthday present; a high quality food churner or whatever it's called. After thirty five years my other half has apparently not cottoned on to the fact that I hate cooking.

The pure creamy mixture is ready. Now, what flavour to impress him with, for believe me, I mean to impress. A slurp of vanilla essence, a tinge of coffee granules, perhaps a bit of seasoning, I think, as I grind pepper and garlic into the large mixing bowl. I spoon in three spoonfuls of curry powder and some almond flavouring and carefully place my little treasure in the oven. The aroma is rather powerful so I open the back door to let in the fresh air.

I decorate my handiwork with thick sweet icing and a zest of lemon and in true traditional style I cram 56 birthday candles onto the, *what now is a crowded*, surface.

"I'm home munchkins. Where's the pressie?" his voice rings in a happy tone.

"I've baked you a special treat. When you've had a cuppa and a taste, then you get your present." I smile a little smile.

He cuts a huge slice to match his growing waist line.

"What a taste!" With a smack of his lips he says with relish, "I could eat it all. That's the best I've ever tasted. What a wife!"

I watch unbelieving as he licks his fingers and presses them to his plate. I watch him savour every last crumb. He still doesn't know how I hate cooking. Then I remember his present and smile. I reach behind the sofa and bring out his present. His bulgy little eyes light up with greed and he rips off the paper of the carefully wrapped parcel, to reveal Delia's "How to Cook" books one and two.

Chantal

Working in the remote high tech laboratories just outside Inverness, Chantal Lyon was a quiet but valued member of the community. She was a bit of an enigma to the other researchers as she often went off on her own and yet she was not unsociable. She knew the right things to say to cheer people up or to give encouragement, but she didn't go out partying and nobody had ever seen her drunk. She was not quite beautiful as she had a strong jaw line but her eyes were large and deep and held attention and she had shiny black hair, like polished ebony. She wore bright red lipstick which matched her immaculate nails and her shapely legs were set off well in high thin stilettos.

Chantal had grown up following in her father's scientific footsteps, although she had never known her father. He had died before she was born. He was doing research into DNA and using cross human-animal embryos to see if there was any way to control Alzheimer's in an aging population. Although slightly unorthodox, he was well enough liked by his colleagues and adored by women. When his body was found, it was thought to have been mauled by a wild panther, so it hit the National news headlines.

There was little evidence, although lots of rumours, that there were wild panthers in Scotland. Several people claimed to have seen them but the few photographs that had been produced were inconclusive. However the coroner found that the injuries to Doctor Lyon were consistent with those of being mauled by a panther.

Chantal's mother had died giving birth and so she had been brought up, without love or affection, by an aunt who had felt it her duty to care for this orphaned member of the family. In spite of this background Chantal grew up and thrived. She was a high achieving scientist in her own right by the time she was twenty-eight.

The director of the research institute informed his staff that they must attend a government briefing on Saturday in Fort William's town hall and her colleague Simon Fortesque offered to drive Chantal. He was a tall dark and good looking man who had never shown any interest in the women at the research centre, but was well known for his inappropriate and often inebriated behaviour in Inverness. This was not something that was held against him by the locals, as being able to have a good drink was a respected part of life these days.

Chantal had hoped to be home by six in the evening but she couldn't get Simon away from the buffet that was served after the meeting. Finally they got into the car. It was quite a way into the journey that Simon, forgetting that he never mixed work and women, made a very clumsy pass at Chantal. She could feel the blood boil under her skin and knew the dangers she risked.

"Stop the car," she demanded. "I want to get out now."

"You can't. We're in the middle of nowhere and it's getting dark," he said. "Look I'm sorry I made that suggestion. I promise I won't touch you."

"I said, STOP THE CAR."

Simon gave in and pulled the car into the side of the road. Normally he did not have this effect on women and even though he had been rejected he felt uneasy about letting her out on her own in the middle of nowhere. He tried one last time,

"Look just let me drop you off in Inverness."

Chantal ignored him. She swung the car door open elegantly and climbed out of the low seat. When he turned to look at her as he drove away, she was gone. It was as if she had vaporized into the twilight.

It was not until Simon was getting out of his car at his home that he noticed the passenger seat had been ripped. "Bitch," he thought, "she'll pay for that".

Meanwhile Chantal was walking along the completely deserted road. All her senses were heightened. The utter loneliness of the place struck her. The light of the day was almost gone and there were no street lamps. She was pleased that there was light from the full moon. It struck her that she really was miles from anywhere and it was going to be a long night. Maybe she should have stayed in Simon's car, but she couldn't be too careful.

A haunting high screeching sound from a fox broke the silence and startled her but she took a deep breath and carried on. She could smell the freshness of the night. This was no different from all the other trials she'd had to face in her life. She just had to get on with it. The road was leading through a thick dark wood, which held many moving deep shadows. Fleetingly she wondered about her father. "Had it been in this sort of countryside that he had died? Had he been trying to trap a panther?"

There was a rustling of leaves and the sound of soft footfalls. By now the adrenaline was racing around Chantal's body. Her eyes glittered in the darkness and she increased her walking pace.

The fox again called in the night and Chantal clearly heard twigs crunch in the shadowy undergrowth. She ran her hands through her sleek black hair and tried to make her breath even. She was going to get through this night.

After two more miles Chantal discarded her shoes. She found that walking on the road, barefoot was actually quite comfortable and certainly she could move much more quickly. Suddenly standing before her was a large black cat. It certainly was not a domestic cat. "So this is how it would be," she thought, "miles from anywhere, just like my father". Not knowing whether to run but realizing even if she could make it up a tree, so would the cat, she stood still and stared at him. She recognised his beauty, even as she recognised his power. They both stood still and stared. There was no way out, but suddenly he moved, stealthily and slowly and skirted around her, always keeping his eyes on her. Then he was gone.

Chantal only started to move when she could see him no more. She drew herself up to her full height and quickly marched onwards. "Perhaps he had recently eaten," she thought.

There were no cars driving past and gradually Chantal relaxed into the night. She was pleased with her fitness and knew that she could walk all night long. In the distance she heard the rumble of a car's engine. Her senses became alert. Should she flag down the car or dive for the undercover of the woods? The car was slowing and she could see the silhouette of a woman. She was not going to get in this woman's car. Why would a woman alone stop and offer a stranger a lift? No she would trust her instincts.

The woman looked out of the window and said, "Do you need a lift?"

"Do I look like I need a lift?" Chantal hissed aggressively. The woman stepped on the accelerator and shot off.

Chantal knew she had made the right decision, especially when three miles later she came across a parked lorry. She felt the adrenaline surge and all her sense prickle. She could hear every little noise as she crept up and peeked through the cab window.

The driver was fast asleep in a hammock type bed, totally oblivious to being spied upon. Chantal stepped down again, slipped off her T- shirt and hid it under a tree and went back to the cab door and banged loudly.

Her heart was thumping hard in her chest, and she could feel the blood rushing through her brain.

When the driver opened the door, she said, "Can you help me with this? I need you to take a look."

The driver eagerly leapt down from the cab. She smiled. It wouldn't hurt to play with him a bit as she beckoned him towards the woods. She leaned forward as if to kiss him, and then the attack began. She sank her teeth into his neck and her hands with their long lacquered nails sunk into his flesh. He was no match for her although he fought for a while. Her powerful jaw ripped at his throat and the blood spurted and dribbled and oozed.

The driver's look of surprise was lost on Chantal as she was immersed in her own world. Suddenly as if by some unexplained charm it started to pour with rain and she threw back her head and embarrassed the wetness. She left the carcass in the grass by the road and out of the corner of her eye she noticed a dark shadow take over where she had left off.

The rain washed away all the crimson debris and she picked up her T-shirt from under the tree and climbed into the cab.

Leaving the nameless driver and his shadowy companion she drove the lorry to the outskirts of Inverness, where she set it alight.

"Morning," she said brightly to Simon as she passed his desk. He had been going to tackle her about his car seat but something about her stopped him. He had just read how a man had been found mauled and half eaten on the road he had left her on last night. She was looking sleek and alert. Her black hair shining and smooth and he noticed for the first time how well she moved.

"Morning, you got back ok I see."
"Oh yes, it was fine." She smiled. She could smell his fear.

Chantal sat down in her office. She had often wondered why her aunt had never loved her, but she was beginning to understand. Of course there was no doubt that she was human, but she realized that her humanness had been enhanced, probably by her father, as one of his own private experiments. She had her father's brains and enough femininity from her mother to make her attractive. Chantal knew she also had reason and choices. These were signs that she was part of the human race. Her mother had died in childbirth because she, the baby was not just a normal baby. She must get hold of her father's notes from the archives. She knew that there were times in the past when she'd had difficulty in stopping herself killing things but last night she'd been in control. She'd not killed her colleague, which would have caused a lot of questions. She'd not dived into a stranger's car. She'd waited until the time was right and she could set up the kill. The scientist in her thought about trying to find ways to curtail her urges but she knew now that she could control it. She'd suppressed her needs for so long and now she wanted to stay who she was; as long as she only indulged herself occasionally!

Recurring Nightmare

"Yes, how can I help you?" Sheila asked the young woman standing at her front door, as she dried her hands on the dishcloth. The young woman, probably no more than sixteen, visibly took a deep breath and then spoke in a clear voice.

"Excuse me for bothering you, but are you Sheila Warren?"

Sheila paused. She had not been called Warren for the last 14 years. "Perhaps you could tell me who you are and why you want to know?"

"My name is Trudy Belling and I am trying to trace Sheila Warren on behalf of a friend who is desperately ill. Before I say any more I really would like to know if I am speaking to the right person."

"I was Sheila Warren, but I married, sometime ago. We'll go and sit on the garden seat and you can tell me more, but I have to tell you I really don't have much time. The children are due home from school within the hour."

The bench was tucked under the shade of a graceful willow tree in the large front garden, but reassuringly in view of the busy pavement. Sheila grabbed her front door keys and led the way.

"We shouldn't be disturbed here, so you can tell me what it is you want."

Trudy took another nervous breath, "My friend is adopted." She paused and looked carefully at Sheila, who did her best to blank her face of all emotion. "I think you are her mother."

Sheila said nothing. Fleetingly she wondered if this woman was speaking on behalf of her daughter or was in fact her daughter? Sheila felt no recognition. There was no obvious family resemblance. No, this was a stranger.

Eventually she said, "So supposing I am, what does she want?"

"There is no easy way to tell you this. Mia is very ill. She has Leukaemia. The doctors have tried everything but what Mia needs is bone marrow from a compatible donor. A relative would be the best bet."

There was so much to take in. They had called her daughter Mia and with that name the shadowy figure that had been at the back of her life became real. She had been relieved to give away her baby. Her daughter was now very ill and who had the power to totally disrupt the safe life she had created for herself. In fact just like that brute had torn away her innocence that terrifying night, her daughter could completely wreck her life now.

Several years after the night that changed her forever Sheila had decided she must just get on with her life. She married Daniel who had always followed her around at school. Now he was a successful banker and although he was very quiet and reserved they had built a good life. If their life lacked love, passion and highs it also lacked lows. She had never pretended to love Daniel and he had never expected it, but they had two lovely boys and a safe, comfortable home.

Trudy was looking uncomfortable. Sheila realized she was not making the expected responses.

"How long has she been ill?" Sheila asked.

"She was diagnosed some months ago. Please help her. I said I would not beg, but she is my best friend. You'd be very proud of her. Everyone loves her."

Sheila said nothing. Her mind was racing. Did she owe Mia anything?

"Perhaps you could contact her father. He could be a possible donor too." Trudy continued, oblivious to the impossibility of the situation.

There was no way she was going to tell Mia about her father. Sheila had no idea, who he was, because he'd worn a balaclava and never been caught. How would the girl get over the knowledge of her beginning? Suddenly she thought of her boys and all their liveliness and potential. She knew that Mia deserved the same chance of a future.

"Write down the hospital I need to go to. Tomorrow I was taking my parents to the garden centre, but I'll tell them what's happened they'll be there too."

She did not tell Daniel about Trudy's visit because she did not want to remind him what had happened to her.

Walking up the steps of the hospital Sheila realized that she was holding her breath. Her father squeezed her arm. They were shown into a magnolia painted waiting room until the doctor was ready to see them. He explained about the blood tests and the need to find a compatible donor.

Sheila hesitated outside the ward trying to pluck up courage to go in. As she walked through the door the couple by Mia's bed smiled and said they were off to the canteen.

There she was after all these years; her daughter! She recognized her immediately and the pounding she was feeling in her chest was almost overpowering. The paleness of her daughter's skin and her apparent fragility made Sheila make the effort to speak to Mia.

"I'm sorry to be meeting you in these circumstances."

"No, thanks for coming."

"It's going to be alright you know. There are several potential donors."

They spent a little while together and then Sheila promised to visit the following day.

After dropping off her parents at their house, she went home and packed a bag for herself and her boys. Then she picked up her children from school and took them to their grandparents.

Through no fault of her own Mia had smashed Sheila's safe life. She was now in a nightmare situation. She went to the police station and the officer who had been in charge of her case was still in the station, albeit at a promoted rank.

That evening when he was arrested, Chief Inspector Battle assured Sheila that she did not have to see him, but Sheila agreed to.

"How can you accuse me of such a thing?" Daniel asked.

"Because after all this time, I know. There is no point in lying anymore and I have absolute proof."

"You can't have, because I didn't do it."

"Today I went to visit the baby that I gave away. She's very seriously ill and needs a bone marrow donor. I expected that there would be some family likeness. That I'd feel some familiarity but do you know what I saw?"

There was silence so Sheila continued. "I saw a very sick young woman who was your spitting image. Your eyes. The shape of your face. Your colouring. Shall I go on?"

"You need to think about what you're saying. What about the boys? What about all the years we've been together? Don't they count for anything?"

"Oh yes, I had one night of pure terror, which has haunted me everyday since and now I know that the monster who did that to me has lived with me for the last twelve years and is the father of my children. How will I ever get that out of my head? You, not I, have damaged us all. I want him prosecuted Chief Inspector."

"Look I made a mistake but we have a good life. You're my wife. You can't do this to our family."

"Now that you've admitted it, you will be charged," interrupted Chief Inspector Battle. "We will of course be collecting DNA samples from you and your daughter, to make sure that the case id foolproof in court."

Sheila turned waked out of the room. Daniel had taken all those years but finally she understood what had happened. She realized he had always been obsessed with her. She could not let him off because she needed time away from him to rebuild their lives and she understood that if he was free, he would never leave them alone. While he was away there would be time to help Mia and then they would set up home elsewhere. Suddenly she felt a huge relief. It was over.

Rochelle's Diary

Saturday 7 June

Today has been like every other day. Mother has her "needs" and I was left to look after Mollie and Angus. "Rochelle take the children to the park for half an hour. There's a good girl," she said in her shrill voice. Of course when I got back she was zonked out on the sofa and the gin bottle was lying on the floor. I don't mind looking after the kids but it would be good if just one day mother cooked a meal or took us out.

And there are things I can't do. For instance today Mollie needed a plaster for her foot and we didn't have any. I looked in all the usual places to see if I could find some money to go and get her some, but I couldn't find any. It's her shoes that are the problem. They're pinching her feet because they're just that bit too small. Maybe I can find her some of my old ones that would fit her better.

We hid behind the sofa when that nasty man came for his money again today. Mother was still out of it so she didn't answer the door and after a lot of banging on the door he went away.

One exciting thing did happen today. The postman bought ME a letter. It was from François, who's my father, but I can't remember him. He wrote to say he's coming to see me. I haven't told mother.

Sunday 8 June

I cleaned up sick from the carpet this morning. It was disgusting. It's the second time lately that mother has just been sick and gone to bed. It was gross and I wanted to just shut the door, but the kids have got to have somewhere to play. I found some disinfectant under the sink and put loads on the carpet after I'd cleaned it. Not sure which smell was worse. The money man doesn't come round on Sundays so I opened all the windows and luckily it was a bright day.

The kids didn't say anything. They never really grumble. I was all set for an awful day when I found there was nothing in the fridge and then I looked in the biscuit tin and found a tenner. When I first saw the pink note at the bottom of the tin I can't tell you how it cheered me up. Mother wasn't up, so we all snuck out to the corner shop and I got a large packet of cereal, some milk, three loaves of bread, a couple of tins of baked beans and a huge chunk of cheese. One good thing about mother these days is she won't remember there was money in the tin and if I get some food with it we can last for a few days. I even bought the kids some chocolate. That was naughty but I thought they deserved it.

Mother surfaced around four but she wasn't really with it. I asked her if she was going to have a bath and she told me not to be cheeky but she did make it to the bathroom. Mollie, Angus and I went through all the piles of old junk in the spare room and I found a pair of half decent shoes that fitted Mollie. She was well chuffed.

Monday 9 June

I didn't see mother before we left for school today, but we were on time. We all went in the shower and then had some cornflakes and milk. We dropped Mollie at her nursery just before nine and then Angus and I ran across the playground to get to our classes on time.

Angus was very quiet. He finds school hard because some of the other kids are not very kind to him. I think of Angus a bit like a shadow. I know shadows are dark but he's like a pale shadow. He sort of merges into the background and people don't notice him until he moves. I wish life wasn't so hard for him.

Still we were all happy at lunchtime. Cook had made our favourite stew and potatoes followed by apple crumble. Lots of the kids don't like the stew. They want hamburgers and pizzas but we all like stew. We all eat in the big hall for our meals and we managed to sit together. Cook let us go back to the hatch to get seconds. She said she had to get rid of it so we might as well eat it up. Then we had crumble. We were all so stuffed and happy that we could hardly move. Luckily none of us had games in the afternoon.

Mother was up when we got home. She was crying because the money man had been in and shouted at her. She had a drink to steady her nerves and was better after that.

Tuesday 10 June

Not a good start to the day. Angus needed his PE shorts and I just couldn't find them anywhere. I tried to wake mother but she groaned at me and told me to go away. Angus didn't want to go to school without them he was so upset. In the end I had to tell him I'd go and tell the teacher it was my fault.

Mrs Harvey is very prim and strict, not my image of what a reception teacher should be. I don't really like her because she's quite scary but I couldn't show Angus that. Actually Mrs Harvey was ok about it. I went and told her I was sorry for losing the PE shorts and it was my fault not my brother's and asked if she wanted me to do a detention. She actually said that I shouldn't worry and went found a spare pair that had been left behind last year. Angus was so relieved and I didn't like to tell her they were much nicer than the ones we'd lost. I even managed to get back to my class before the bell went.

My teacher, Mr Simms wasn't too kind today though. He said my homework was very scrappy and couldn't I have made the effort to type it up. Still cook gave me an extra potion of potatoes at lunch because she said I had given her a lovely smile. She's very easily pleased.

Wednesday 11 June

I was quite nervous about bunking off school, especially as I had to get Mollie and Angus in and then slip out again. François was coming to see me today. I hadn't told mother because I knew she'd say no. Mother was still asleep when he arrived and I explained that I had to be home by 3pm so I could pick the others up from school. Francois said that wasn't my job and I shouldn't worry about it. I knew he wasn't going to get me back in time so I nipped next door and persuaded Mrs Partridge to pick them up. She's a good sort and I only ask her help when it's really needed.

François drove us to Beeston Castle. It was a bit frightening being with someone you don't know but I didn't have too much time to worry as the climb to the top was quite steep. He asked me loads of questions but when it was lunchtime there were some very awkward silences.

In the afternoon he told me all about the castle and we looked out at the views right over to Liverpool. He did make it sound interesting but perhaps that was because he had a funny accent. In the afternoon we found a sloping bit of grass and he surprised me by suggesting we did roly-polys down it. We did laugh. I quite liked him really but he wasn't that interested in Mollie or Angus because they aren't his.

Thursday 12 June

After school I was sitting looking out of the window, mother was more sober than I'd seen her for quite some time, and I saw François roll up in his car. Luckily I rushed out to meet him and when I did he presented me with a dog. I was so cross with him. I shouted and raged at him. How were we supposed to feed a dog when we sometimes didn't have enough food for us? On and on I ranted. I just couldn't stop. I said to him who did he think would look after the puppy while we were at school. Was he mad? I told him how mother had her needs and he had to take the puppy back before Mollie and Angus saw him. They'd want to keep him and we just couldn't.

I'm sitting here with my head in my hands. How could I have been so rude? He will never come back. His skin went white with rage and he didn't say a word. He just climbed back in the car with the puppy. I'll never see him again.

Friday 13 June

Don't believe all they say about Friday 13. They can be good days. François arrived as Mollie, Angus and I were finishing the last of the cornflakes. He said that he wished to speak to mother, who of course was still in bed. I said we had to get to school so he took us in his car. All the children in my class noticed and Angus was actually smiling as he went through the gates.

After school mother and he came to pick us up from school. She actually looked quite good. I'd like to say that there is a happy ever after ending but it's not quite like that. By the time we got home from school the spare room had been completely cleaned out and François told us that he was going to be a lodger in our house for the next few months.

We sat down to eat together that evening. It was a wonderful meal of steak and chips. Mollie and Angus were really taken with François and mother was making a big effort. When I was washing up with François later he said I was his little rock; someone sensible and reliable. Apparently that's what my name means.

While I'm sitting here writing my diary I can hear mother singing to Mollie and Angus, "Speed Bonnie Boat" and I can remember back all those years ago when she used to sing to me. It makes me smile.

I know life won't be easy. Mother has a lot to deal with and maybe François won't stay around too long but for the first time in ages I'm feeling hopeful.

Christmas Feelings

It was that time of year again. Christine ignored the "Christmas Ideas" shop that had opened in the shopping centre in September and the large Santas and displays that sprung up throughout October. When the lights were strung precariously across the busy main road she shut her eyes, but now there were five shopping days to Christmas and it could be ignored no longer.

She had no wish to celebrate Christmas. Nigel would be spending his first Christmas with his new wife and quite a few of the people she regarded as her friends would be visiting them. Her close friends, those she loved and cared about, had all asked her over for Christmas, either to stay or to spend the day, but she shamelessly lied and said she was going away. There was no way she was going to pretend to be happy this year.

Christine did all the things that were expected. She sent cards to everyone and bought the required presents. In the window of her front room she placed a tiny Christmas tree with lights and her old fairy rag doll, so that everyone could see that she was back to normal, which of course she was not.

There was one thing positive about being single again, after all these years and that was she would not have to cook that huge meal that took so long to prepare and was demolished so quickly. Nigel had never believed in helping in the kitchen and it always seemed easier to do it all than to have rows. Christine decided that for her Christmas meal she would have a special nut roast, which came with a rich mushroom sauce and lots of fresh vegetables. She quite liked the idea of becoming vegetarian. She added a couple of bottles of her favourite wine to the shopping basket and a rich chocolate sponge pudding. Now that she didn't have to spend a small fortune on Nigel's present there was enough to treat herself a bit. She bought herself a couple of books by her favourite authors and a box set of Lord of the Rings DVD. That should be enough to keep her occupied for Christmas and Boxing Day. In fact it would be quite pleasant.

On impulse she also treated herself to a new outfit. The russet colour suited her deep brown hair and brought out the richness of her large green eyes. It was a long time since she had bought such a beautiful dress.

When Christmas morning dawned, she was on her own. The house was silent and nothing needed to be done. She almost wished she had accepted one of the offers to visit her friends. Outside the sky was grey and the rain was relentless. On an impulse she decided to go to church and briskly marched up the road with her large umbrella clutched tightly against the wind.

As she approached the church the bells were ringing. It was a really beautiful sound and lifted her spirits. She reached the open door of the church and saw that it was actually a CD player was belting out the noise. "Happy Christmas," greeted old Mrs Marshall, who organised everything at the church. It was a warm welcome and Christine's smiled.

"Did you like my idea for the bells?" Mrs Marshall asked. "We couldn't get anyone to bell ring this morning."

Christine could feel a little giggle rising in her throat. She thought it was hilarious to have the bells on CD. "A novel idea, Mrs Marshall and a very happy Christmas to you too."

The service was a happy event, with the congregation singing lots of lovely traditional hymns and everyone being friendly. As the service was ending the vicar announced that Mrs Marshall had a notice.

"There are nine parishioners who would've been on their own this Christmas who are coming to me for dinner. My daughter was coming over to help me and unfortunately, for reasons I won't bore you with, she can't make it. I know I can cope, but if anyone could come over and just help for an hour it would be so appreciated. Thank you."

The church emptied and everyone took a few moments to chat and went on their way.

Christine thought of her lovely meal, but Mrs Marshall was too old to be left to cope with such a large catering job on her own, so she volunteered to pop along and help. The two of them tackled the last bits of preparation. The meat was cooking and vegetables were all prepared. Soon the parishioners arrived and Christine bustled round serving drinks, washing up, serving food, pulling crackers and listening to the appalling jokes. She even found herself laughing.

Later she tackled the bulk of the washing up with Mr Owen, an octogenarian, who made several quite improper proposals to her. By four o'clock the well fed group were dozing off and Christine slipped away to her home for her long awaited meal. It had been a good day, with lots of amusement and kindness and she felt useful again.

She popped her nut roast into the oven, poured an extra large glass of chilled wine and settled down to read a chapter of one of her new books, but as she sat down she noticed the answer phone was flashing. It was probably her son calling from Australia to wish her a Happy Christmas. Christine hit the button.

"Hi Mum, I don't know whether you want to know this, but I've just had a call from Chester Hospital. Dad is going to be alright, but he and Tracy have been taken to hospital with food poisoning. Can you believe it? Apparently their turkey wasn't defrosted properly. Anyway I thought you ought to know. I'm not sure why. I hope you're having a better Christmas than Dad. I'll try and call later. Love from us all here."

Christine took a moment to think how this news made her feel. Tracy may be young and beautiful but she had probably been left to cook a huge turkey without any help. You learned so much as you grew older. She was glad that Nigel and Tracey were not in any danger and suddenly life seemed clearer. There was no need to wish for the past. She had a lovely home, wonderful children and many skills. She had really enjoyed helping out today. Christine picked up the phone and called her oldest friend. She wished her a very merry Christmas and said that she would after all, like to take up her invitation for lunch on Boxing Day. She'd wear her new dress. Then she settled down to enjoy her evening.